A DIAMOND FOR
THE SINGLE MUM

A DIAMOND FOR THE SINGLE MUM

SUSAN MEIER

MILLS & BOON

First published in Great Britain 2018
by Mills & Boon, an imprint of HarperCollins*Publishers*
1 London Bridge Street, London, SE1 9GF

Large Print edition 2019

© 2018 Linda Susan Meier

ISBN: 978-0-263-08233-3

MIX
Paper from
responsible sources
FSC® C007454

This book is produced from independently certified FSC™ paper to ensure responsible forest management. For more information visit www.harpercollins.co.uk/green.

Printed and bound in Great Britain
by CPI Group (UK) Ltd, Croydon, CR0 4YY

For my son, Michael.
I'll probably miss you forever.

CHAPTER ONE

HARPER SLOAN HARGRAVES looked up at the condo building looming before her. Nestled in the heart of Manhattan, the tall structure gleamed in the early morning sun of a warm September day. Black trim enhanced the grey brick exterior. Leafy green trees decorated the courtyard, along with topiary roses in enormous ceramic pots.

Well-dressed men and women ambled out of the wide, tinted-glass door and bobbed along the street on their way to undoubtedly prestigious jobs. Taxis, town cars and limos rolled by— quietly, to match the clean, subdued area around her.

Fighting the urge to glance down at her torn jeans and simple T-shirt, Harper tightened her fingers on the handle of her daughter's stroller and gave it a quick push toward the door. It opened automatically, revealing the kind of lobby typically reserved for luxury resorts but borrowed for the rarefied world of New York City's upwardly mobile. The tinkling of the falling-rain fountain in the center of the room greeted her. Gray-and-white-print area rugs highlighted black slate floors. A stainless-steel banister on the ultramodern stairway, steel elevator doors and steel window frames sharpened gray walls. Green plants sat discreetly in corners, while vases of red and purple flowers added pops of color.

"Can I help you?"

A doorman. Of course. She hadn't expected otherwise. At one time, Harper had belonged in a building like this one. She'd grown up in an area so lush she'd taken luxury for granted and had rejected it. Then she'd married Clark Hargraves and fallen into the lap of luxury again, only to lose it all when he'd died.

She'd been rich, then poor, then rich again. Now, she had no idea who or what she was.

She walked up to the shiny black desk where the doorman stood staring at her. "I'm here to see Seth McCallan."

Wearing a red sweater with the gray building logo in the upper left-hand corner, the doorman straightened. "Mr. McCallan will be leaving for work in a few minutes. Is he expecting you?"

She'd known seeing Seth wouldn't be easy. He was one of *the* McCallans. Owners of enough Manhattan real estate to be unofficial royalty, though he'd been a penniless student when he'd met Clark. He'd renounced his family and their money and had been forced to move into Clark's run-down apartment with him. Two years after they'd graduated, Seth had persuaded him to start an investment firm together. Five successful years later, he'd gotten Clark accustomed to being somebody, then decided to help his brother with the family's business and sold his share of the investment firm to Clark.

It all seemed so generous, except Clark had spent every cent he'd made keeping up the facade that he and Harper were as wealthy as Seth. He didn't have the money to buy Seth's share, so he'd leveraged the firm. And mortgaged their condo.

She'd had to sell both after he'd died to pay off the bank.

"He's not expecting me, but I'm a personal friend."

And he owes me, she thought, her chin raising. If he'd kept his share of their investment firm, not forced Clark to mortgage everything they owned, she wouldn't be desperate right now.

Keeping his eyes on her, the doorman picked up his house phone.

"Mr. McCallan, you have a visitor. Harper Hargraves." A pause. "Yes. I'll be happy to send her up."

The doorman motioned to the elevator. She headed to the shiny steel door, and he followed her. When the door opened, he directed her to go inside and walked in with her.

He was keeping tabs on her. Making sure the scraggly woman with the baby didn't go anywhere else in the building.

Humiliation burned through her.

When the car stopped at the ninth floor, he didn't accompany her out, but stood waiting in the elevator as she rolled her stroller to Seth's door, then knocked.

The door opened, and Harper forgot all about the doorman watching her. Her husband's former best friend stood before her in a pair of gray sweatpants that hung low on his hips, as he wrestled a T-shirt over his head. He yanked the thing down his torso, but it was too late. She'd seen the rippling muscles of his chest and stomach.

Shell-shocked, she stared at him. He was taller, sleeker, more muscular than he had been five years ago. But with his perpetual smile and tousled black hair, he was the same heart-stopping handsome he'd been when they lived in side-by-side apartments. And those eyes of his. As black as the soul of a condemned man, they nonetheless had a strange light. Almost a knowing. As if the years had taught him to be careful...wise. Though he'd been a nervous nerd when he'd lived with Clark, he seemed to have found his confidence as a man.

It was easy to see why the tabloids gossiped about him being with a different woman every few weeks. Confident. Rich. Handsome. Built. He had everything—

Which she shouldn't be noticing. She'd had the love of her life. Their marriage had been fun, perfect. She missed Clark with every fiber of her being.

"Hey, Seth."

His gaze ran from her short cap of black hair down her simple T-shirt, along her worn jeans and back up again.

"Harper?"

She tried to smile. "It's me. I know I look a little different."

"A little different" didn't hit the tip of the iceberg. Since Clark's funeral, she'd had a baby, cut her long black hair and lost weight. She was suddenly grateful for the supercilious doorman. If he hadn't announced her, Seth might not have recognized her.

He gestured awkwardly. "I've never seen the baby."

"Her name is Crystal." Her words came out on a shaky breath, and she knew she had to get this over with before she lost her courage. "I need some help."

"I guessed that from the fact that you're here at eight o'clock on a Tuesday." He stepped back so she could enter. "Come in."

He held the door for the stroller. As Harper slipped by, her gaze flicked down his torso again. He looked so good in T-shirt and sweats. Fit. Agile.

Maybe a little intimidating.

That was probably why she kept noticing. Not interest. Fear. She'd never asked anyone for help. Never. She'd always made it on her own.

She pushed the stroller into the living room of the sophisticated open-floorplan condo. Motioning to the aqua sofa, Seth indicated she should sit, as he lowered himself to the matching trellis-print chair. She could see the white cabinets in the kitchen, along with a restored wood dining table surrounded by six tufted chairs the same color as the sofa, with a modern chandelier hanging overhead. Simple, but luxurious. Rich fabrics. Expensive wood. Even when a McCallan lived simply, he did it with understated elegance.

"I'm sorry to bother you, but I'm in a bit of a bind. I sold my condo yesterday, but the buyer wants it on Monday."

"That's great? Good? Awful?" He shook his head. "It's been too long. I'm not sure what to say."

She laughed, so nervous she couldn't even react normally around him. "It would be great, except I don't have another place to move into."

"Oh."

"The buyer paid cash and getting the place in a week was a condition of the sale and I really needed the sale…so I took the offer."

"You need money?" He frowned. "You own an investment firm."

And here was the tough part. Her wonderful, funny, smart husband had done what he'd had to do to buy Seth's share. Had he lived, that loan would have been a footnote in his life story. As it was, it had all but destroyed his legacy. The last thing in the world she wanted to do was tell Clark's best friend that he'd failed—

No, the last thing in the world she wanted to do was tell *her parents* Clark had failed. Seth, at least, would give Clark the benefit of the doubt. Her parents—her *mother*—would have a royal fit, then belittle Clark every time Harper mentioned his name.

"I had to sell the firm. Clark had leveraged it to get the money to buy your share and the market plummeted. It was like a perfect storm, Seth. I couldn't pay the loan and I couldn't sell the firm until I dropped the price to a few hundred thousand dollars over the amount we owed." She shifted the focus of Seth's disappointment from Clark to her. "And that money's almost gone because I needed it for living expenses while I had the baby and waited to sell the condo."

A hush fell over the room. Harper refused to say anything more. He might not belittle Clark the way her mom would when Harper finally told her parents she was broke, but Seth was an entitled rich kid. He'd dropped out of his family for a while, but when he and Clark had graduated university, Seth had used his connections to land them jobs in an investment firm. He'd gotten family friends to pony up the starting funds when he and Clark wanted to open their own company. When the business was more than on its feet, he'd found the money to buy out their investors. And when he needed to go to work for his family's company, after his dad's death, he'd easily handed over the firm's reins to Clark, not caring that he was giving up what could have been a gold mine if he and Clark had stayed around to run it.

Seth might have lived poor for a few years while he finished school, but he had no concept of genuine, lifelong struggle. And Harper wouldn't let him think less of Clark because he'd lost what he and Seth had built.

After a few seconds, Seth sighed. "And you sold your condo because that was mortgaged, too?"

"I didn't realize until after Clark died that we'd spent every penny he'd earned." She gave him time to digest that, then added, "He really liked you. He liked the life you brought him into. I know why he overextended us financially. And I'm not sorry he lived the way he wanted to while he had a chance. I'm not asking for anything except some help figuring my way out of this. Some advice."

"Even if you rent, you're going to need more than a week to find a place."

"I know."

Three-month-old Crystal stretched. Her head rose above the bundle of blankets she'd been snuggled into, revealing a tiny pixie face and a head full of short, shaggy black hair. Realizing the baby was waking from the stroller-induced nap, Harper slid the diaper bag out of the bin behind the seat. "I'm going to have to warm a bottle."

Seth looked at Crystal. "Is she waking up?"

"Yes. She won't fuss if I have a bottle ready."

He rose, as if confused. "Okay."

"Just let me warm the bottle and I'll be all set."

She took the diaper bag into the kitchen and removed a bottle. As she opened the cupboard door to get something to hold enough water to warm it, she watched Seth peer into the stroller from about six feet away.

"You can actually get close enough to look at her."

Seth grimaced. "Not on your life. I have a

niece a few months older than she is and I've never even held her."

Harper clicked her tongue. "Seth! Babies are wonderful."

"They look like they are. And my brother absolutely adores his. But they're small and fragile and they frequently leak bodily fluids. I'm keeping my distance."

She nodded, grateful for the small reprieve in talking about the mess she'd gotten herself into. She filled a mug with hot water and slid the bottle inside. Knowing it would take a few minutes to warm the formula that way, she walked back into the living room.

Seth said, "She's pretty. Looks a lot like my niece. Dark hair. Pale eyes."

"Sounds like your brother."

He laughed. "He has a talent for getting his own way about things." But Seth's laughter quickly died. His solemn dark eyes met hers. "You do realize how much trouble you're in."

"And you're about to tell me the only answer is to go back to my parents." She shook her head. "That has to be my last resort. My mother was abysmal to Clark until he started that business with you. Then she was constantly on his back to be more, to push for more, to have more. If I go home now and tell her that I not only sold the investment firm, I sold the condo to get out from under loans, she'll lose all respect for him."

Seth silently studied Harper. Still beautiful. Still tempting. And in so much trouble financially he wasn't even sure how to counsel her.

He spent his days haggling with contractors, hammering out contracts with some of the savviest businessmen in the world and fighting to make sure McCallan, Inc. stayed at the top of its industry. Yet he had absolutely no idea what to say to one little woman.

If she were anybody else, he'd easily tell her, "Suck it up, Buttercup. You've got no option but to move back in with your parents."

Except, she wasn't staying away from them for herself. She was holding back, probably waiting until she had herself on solid ground, before she had to tell her parents her husband had put her into debt. She was protecting Clark.

How could someone who'd fought his own condescending father most of his life not respect that?

The baby stirred again. Harper went to the kitchen and got the bottle.

Just as the little girl began to fuss, Harper was back, bottle in hand, lifting Crystal, settling her on her lap and feeding her.

It all seemed to simple, so easy. He'd seen his sister-in-law, Avery, do something similar. But Avery had tons of help. Not just Seth and Jake's mom, but Avery's mom, her dad and a nanny. He'd always thought Avery made being a mom look easy, but he'd apparently missed a lot about parenting in his years of avoiding babies.

"So, I'm kinda broke, but not really," Harper said, feeding the hungry baby. "With the sale of the condo I have a hundred thousand dollars to play with. Either to use for a down payment on a new condo or to live on until I find a job."

He sat back down, feeling oddly foolish for being so persnickety about kids as he watched Harper's baby happily suckle her milk. "Honestly, if you weren't out on the street in six days, I'd say your first order of business should be to get a job."

"But I am out on the street in six days. In that time, I have to pack and arrange for a mover, as

I find somewhere else to live. You wouldn't happen to have an extra room?"

She'd said it as a joke, but he did have an extra room. She'd even have a private bathroom. There were only two problems with taking her in. First, he really wasn't comfortable around babies. Very few single men were. But he was super edgy around them. Preoccupied with a million little details for his job, he worried he'd step on Crystal, trip over her, knock her down.

But he knew that was just a cover for the real reason he didn't want Harper Sloan Hargraves to move in with him.

She was supposed to be his.

He'd adored her from the moment he'd laid eyes on her. But he wasn't the settling-down kind. His parents' farce of a marriage had ruined him on the fairy tale of happily-ever-after. The emotional abuse he'd suffered from his manipulative dad had made him far too cynical and too careful to want a relationship.

So, he'd let Clark ask her out.

And he'd become a playboy. He'd dated so many women he'd lost count. He traveled, was a regular in Las Vegas and couldn't remember the last Saturday night he'd spent alone.

"I was kidding about the room, Seth. You can talk again."

He shook his head. This wasn't about him. It really wasn't even about Harper. It was about Clark. He'd been Seth's best friend in every sense of the word. When he left his family home and his emotionally abusive father, Clark had found him in the library. Alone. Broke. And rich-kid stupid. Seth didn't even know he couldn't hide in the library stacks, wait for the lights to go out and spend the night. He didn't notice things like cameras and security guards.

Clark had asked a few pointed questions, gotten the real scoop and taken him to the run-down apartment he shared with Ziggy, next door to Harper. He'd told him he could stay until he got on his feet, but for three kids going to university, fighting for money for books and tuition, there was no getting on any feet. He'd found a job as a waiter, shared a room with twin beds with Ziggy and paid his part of the rent and food.

All his life, his dad had told him he didn't understand the real world and tried to teach him by withholding money, embarrassing him, belittling him, and Clark had taught him everything his dad couldn't in three years of paying for school and supporting himself.

Now here he was with an extra room, about to turn Clark's widow out on the street because he'd at one time had a crush on her?

That was ridiculous. He was a grown man now. A wealthy man in his own right who'd built exactly the life he wanted. He had his pick of woman and absolutely no desire to settle down.

She was safe…and so was he.

"You can have the room."

"What?"

He rose from the trellis-print chair. "You can have my spare room. Arrange to have your furniture put into storage. Have Crystal's crib delivered here." And just as Clark had said to him twelve years ago, he added, "You can stay as long as you need to."

CHAPTER TWO

HARPER BLINKED. "WHAT?"

"I'm offering you a place to stay. Clark took me in when I was in trouble. I owe him."

"Okay. But, Seth, as beautiful as your condo is, it's small and Crystal can be very noisy."

He walked toward the kitchen and the coffee-maker. "And I'm not home a lot. I work from nine to six. Most evenings I have dinner meetings or dates. You're going to find you have the condo to yourself more than you think."

She didn't know why that gave her a funny feeling in the pit of her stomach.

He made his coffee, then glanced at his watch. "I have just enough time to get ready for work." He motioned to the door. "You go home, get things settled and come back when you need to. I'll have keys made for you."

She slid Crystal into the stroller. "Are you sure?"

He smiled. Harper's heart thumped. The grown-up version of Clark's best friend was absolutely gorgeous.

"This is not a big deal."

Harper totally disagreed. Ten minutes ago, Seth wouldn't get within six feet of her baby. Now he thought he could live with her? Not to mention the way she kept noticing he was attractive, reacting when he smiled. She was lonely and vulnerable, missing Clark, and Seth wasn't known for discretion when it came to women.

Moving in together did not seem like a good idea.

Seth headed back down the hall, probably toward his bedroom. "As soon as you're settled, we'll go over your résumé, find you a job and start house hunting."

Because those were things Clark had helped him with.

He hadn't said it, but she realized this was nothing but payback for Clark's kindnesses and, honestly, she needed it. If her mother saw her, six days away from being homeless, she'd blame Clark and never forget.

Harper could not let that happen.

She said, "Okay," but he was already opening the door of his room.

Harper blew her breath out on a long sigh. This was not going to be easy, but it was better than living in the street.

After spending an hour contacting movers, Harper finally found one who had a cancellation in his schedule the following day. She booked the appointment and spent the rest of the afternoon, evening and the next morning packing. Right on time, the movers arrived and picked up her furniture and boxes of household goods, clothes and baby things. They drove first to the storage unit and dropped off everything but Crystal's crib and baby accessories, which were packed in the back of her SUV with a few suitcases of clothes.

She waved goodbye to the movers and headed for Seth's condo.

Though it was close to five, Seth had told her he worked until six and she knew he wouldn't be home. Which meant she could have everything set up in his condo before he returned.

But when she arrived at his building, the doorman wouldn't let her into Seth's apartment. Not that she blamed him. She'd thought Seth would have already made arrangements, but apparently he hadn't.

The doorman punched a few numbers into his

phone and within seconds was talking to Seth. Then he handed the phone across the desk.

"He wants to talk to you."

Oh, boy. He probably wasn't expecting her until Sunday. Plenty of time for him to get adjusted or change his mind. Instead here she was, a little over twenty-four hours later, her car loaded with baby things.

What did a playboy need with a baby and broke widow?

"Hello. Seth." Not giving him a chance to back out, she said, "I got lucky and found a mover who'd had a cancellation today. I packed last night and this morning, and now everything I own, except Crystal's things and a couple suit-cases of clothes, is in a storage unit."

She hadn't meant to sound desperate, but oh, Lord, she had. She squeezed her eyes shut, but Seth easily said, "Okay."

Her heart started beating again.

"I have one more meeting before I can leave, but I'll call my next-door neighbor, Mrs. Petrillo. She has a key and will let you in. Just go ahead to the condo."

"Should I knock on her door?"

He laughed. "No. She's something of a snoop.

It's why I want her to let you in instead of George. She looks out the keyhole every time the elevator arrives on our floor. This way she'll know I know you're there."

Harper laughed. Her first genuine laugh since she'd realized how much trouble she was in. She liked the idea of a nosy neighbor. It felt less like she and Seth were all alone.

Because they weren't. They had Crystal, the nosy neighbor and probably a hundred other people who lived in the building.

They would not be alone.

"I also have an extra parking space in the basement. I told George to get you a pass."

"Okay. Thanks." When she disconnected the call, George handed her the card that would get her entry into the garage. "Is your car on the street?"

"Yes. I was lucky to get a spot right in front of the building."

"Good. I'll arrange to have your luggage and baby things brought upstairs. Then I'll park your car in Mr. McCallan's second space."

Balancing Crystal on her hip, she wondered how much Seth had promised this guy to be so accommodating. She handed him her car keys. "Thanks. It's the blue Explorer SUV."

He nodded once. "We'll have your things upstairs in a few minutes."

She rode the elevator to Seth's floor and just as Seth had predicted a short gray-haired woman stood by his door, waiting for her.

"Mrs. Petrillo?"

"Yes. And you must be Harper."

"Yes." She presented her baby. "This is Crystal."

The older woman lightly pinched Crystal's pink cheek. "She is adorable. Aren't you, sweetie?"

Crystal grinned.

Mrs. Petrillo inserted the key into the lock and opened the door. "Sorry about your husband."

"Thank you."

"Death is a terrible thing. I buried three husbands."

Harper gasped. Knowing the pain of losing Clark and the emptiness that followed, the loneliness that never seemed to go away, she said, "I'm so sorry."

"It never gets easier." She turned to Harper with a smile. "My soap is on right now. But I'm next door if you need anything."

"Okay. Thanks."

The petite woman waved goodbye and was gone within seconds, but her comment that it would never get easier haunted Harper as a new wave of missing Clark swept through her.

But she barely had time to catch her breath. The doorman arrived with her and Crystal's suitcases.

He led her to the extra room in Seth's condo. A queen-size bed and a dresser easily shared the space, leaving more than ample room for Crystal's crib. An adjoining bathroom with a shower made of black, gray and white glass tiles that matched a backsplash behind the white sink was small but not uncomfortably so.

The doorman left her suitcases on the bed and left. When he returned with the crib and high chair, he had two maintenance men with him. He introduced them, telling her they would set up the crib.

When they were done, Harper put Crystal in her bed to play with her favorite blanket and stuffed bear, and set about to unpack. She hadn't brought a lot, only enough clothes for her and Crystal for two weeks. Everything fit in the one dresser and the small closet. Another indicator of how much her life had changed since she lost Clark.

Not wanting to dwell on that, she carried Crystal to the living space. A quick glance at the clock told her it was only six. Her stomach rumbled. She hadn't eaten lunch. The mover was on too tight of a schedule.

Just when she would have gone into the tidy kitchen to see if there was something she could make for supper, something nice that could serve as a thank-you-for-keeping-us gesture, the condo door opened.

"Seth?"

The day before, she'd left as he'd walked back to his room to dress for work. She expected to see him in a suit, not a black crew-neck sweater with a white shirt under it and jeans.

Jeans to work? At his family's prestigious holding company, where he wasn't just on the board of directors, but was also a vice president?

"I canceled my meeting." He ambled into the room and tossed his keys and wallet on the counter, along with some envelopes she assumed were his mail. "How'd today go?"

She couldn't stop staring at him. Clark had gone to work in a suit and tie every day. He didn't cancel meetings. He never came home early. But Seth was a McCallan. From what she knew of the family, they did whatever they wanted. Especially Seth. Joining the family business obviously hadn't ended his rebellious streak.

"Busy. Exhausting."

He picked up the mail. Rifled through it. "Mine, too."

The conversation ended, and a weird silence stretched between them.

She sucked in a breath for courage. "I was just thinking about looking in your cupboards to see if there was anything to make for dinner."

He sniffed. "Don't bother. I'm pretty sure the cupboards are bare. There are takeout menus from a few local places. Order something for both of us. I have a credit card on file at all of them. Just tell them it's for me." He turned and headed back down the hall.

She frowned. "I thought you'd said you always have dates or dinner meetings or something?"

He stopped, faced her. "I did. Just like I canceled my last meeting, I canceled my date."

Harper blinked as he disappeared behind his bedroom door. *Canceled his date?*

An odd sensation rippled through her. Not happiness. Surely, she couldn't be happy that he'd canceled a date. She didn't "like" the guy. He was good-looking—well, gorgeous, really—but he wasn't Clark, a man she had loved. The feeling oozing through her was more of a recognition of how glad she was that she didn't have to be alone.

The door closed behind Seth and he leaned against it, blowing his breath out on a long sigh. When he'd invited Harper to live with him, he hadn't anticipated how uncomfortable it would be to have her in his house, but he was damn glad he'd canceled his date, so they could talk. About Clark. After a nice dinner, where he'd direct the conversation so she would remind him that she'd loved and married his best friend, he'd get his perspective back.

He took a quick shower. When he left his room and entered the living space, he found Harper at the table surrounded by boxes of Chinese food.

"I like Chinese."

"Good."

He walked over to the table, saw she'd found plates and utensils and took a seat.

"Your area of the city has just about every type of restaurant imaginable."

"It's part of the appeal."

He lifted a dish, filled it with General Tso's chicken, some vegetables and an egg roll.

"Oh, and I paid for it myself. I'm not destitute. And I'm not a charity case. I just need some help transitioning."

Point number one to be discussed. How she wanted to be treated. "I'm sorry if I made you feel that way."

"You didn't. I just wanted to fix some misinterpretations."

"Okay."

She turned her attention to dishing out some food for herself. Her short hair gave her an angelic look, enhanced by the curve of her full lips. Her casual, almost grungy clothes took him back to a decade ago, when he was a kid who listened to hip-hop and lived right next door to the girl he thought the most beautiful woman he'd ever met.

And that was point number two they had to discuss. Eight years had passed since he'd had a crush on her and she'd started dating Clark. They weren't those people anymore. He didn't have a mad crush on *her*. He'd had a mad crush on the girl she'd used to be. Since then, she'd gotten married, lost a husband, had a baby alone. They weren't picking up where they'd left off.

He almost rolled his eyes at his own stupidity. He hadn't even asked how she was.

"So… How are you doing?"

She shook her head. "You mean aside from being almost homeless?"

"Don't make a joke. Clark was my best friend." There. He'd said it. Point number three that he needed to get into this conversation. Clark had been his best friend. "You lost him. You were pregnant. You went through that alone. And now you're facing raising a daughter alone. If we're going to do this—live together—we're going to do it right. Not pretend everything is fine. We used to be friends. We could be friends again."

She set down her chopsticks. "Okay. If you really want to know, I spent most of the year scared to death. It took me a couple of weeks to wrap my head around the fact that he was really gone. But the more I adjusted, the quieter the house got. And the quieter the house got, the more I realized how alone I was."

"And you couldn't even talk to your parents?"

"My mom never had anything good to say

about Clark, so after a visit or two when I was lonely, I quit going over."

She stopped talking, but Seth waited, glad he'd decided to go this route. He needed to know what he was dealing with, and if she'd been alone for twelve long months she probably needed someone to talk to.

"I didn't shut them out completely. My mom came with me to a doctor's appointment or two and then we'd have lunch. But every time, the conversation would turn into a discussion of what I should do with my life now that Clark was gone."

"I'm sorry."

"Not your fault. My mother's a bulldozer. She sees the way a thing should go and she pushes. Whether it's the right thing or not."

"Have they seen the baby?"

"Yes. If I'd completely broken off ties, my mom would have mounted a campaign to get me back. So, I kept them at a distance. I let her stay and help the week after Crystal was born. But she couldn't stop talking about remodeling the condo to bring it up to standards, insinuating that with Clark gone I could do it right, and the whole time I knew I was broke and going to have to sell. Every time I'd try to tell her, she'd blast Clark." She lifted her eyes to catch his gaze. "That's how I knew I couldn't move in with them."

Seth leaned back in his chair. "I guess."

The room got quiet. Her mother wasn't the hellish dictator his father had been, but he wouldn't have wanted to live with her mom, either.

"So, what's up with you?"

He laughed, glad for her obvious change of subject to lighten the mood. "Not much. Jake's a much better businessman than my father was, so working with him is good."

"And your mom?"

He snorted. "My mom isn't quite as bad as your mom, but we have our issues."

She nodded sagely. "Sometimes the best you can do is avoid them for the sake of peace."

He'd never say that the feelings he had around his mother were peaceful. He had a million questions he'd like to ask. Like, why she'd said nothing when his father embarrassed or humiliated him and Jake. Or better yet, why she'd stayed married to a man who was awful as a husband and father? She'd known he was cheating. She'd known he wasn't a good father. Yet she'd stayed. Forcing them all to live a lie.

Deciding he didn't want to burden Harper with any of that, he rose. "Do you like baseball?"

"Sort of."

"Sort of?" He sniffed a laugh. "There's a game on tonight that I'd love to see. If you want to watch, too, I can watch out here. If not, I can watch on the television in my bedroom."

"I don't want you to change your routines for me."

"I won't."

The sound of the baby crying burst from her phone. She held it up. "Baby monitor is attached to this. And it looks like I'm going to be busy for a while. Go ahead and put your game on."

Harper walked into her room sort of happy. It had been nice to talk about Clark, her mom and even being alone. She wasn't trying to make a new best friend, but she had been lonely. Having someone to talk to, to share a meal with, had been more of a treat than she'd expected it would be.

With Crystal on her arm she walked out to the common area and found Seth was nowhere around. Thinking he must have decided to watch the game in his room, she warmed a bottle, fed Crystal, played with her, let her sit in her little seat that rocked her sideways, then finally put her into bed.

After a quick shower, and still wired from their talk, she put on a pair of pajamas and returned to the living room to watch TV.

A few minutes later, Seth returned to the main living area. He held up his phone. "Work call. I also took a shower while I was back there." He set the phone on the center island and pulled a beer from the fridge. "Want one?"

She shook her head. "No. I might have to get up in the middle of the night."

That piece of information seemed to horrify him. "Really?"

"Crystal is a fairly good sleeper, but I never know."

He twisted the top off the bottle. "So, on the off chance that she'll wake up, you don't drink?"

"Yes."

He sat beside her. She liked his hair all rumpled from his shower. Whatever his soap was it made him smell like heaven.

Strange things happened to her pulse. Her

breathing shifted. Probably so she could inhale the wonderful scent of his soap or shampoo.

She eased a few more inches away from him. It didn't help.

"What are you watching?"

She handed him the remote. "Nothing. Put the game on. I need to get to bed."

He frowned.

"You know…in case Chrystal wakes up."

"Right."

She walked into her room and closed the door behind her with a deep sigh. Her weird reactions around him shouldn't surprise her. Her husband had been gone a year and she'd all but locked herself in her house. Primarily to prepare for and then care for her baby. And she might be too needy to be around such a gorgeous guy. But she also couldn't risk slipping it to her parents that Clark had failed. Or, worse, having her mom or dad read her body language, realize something was wrong and grill her until she crumbled. That had kept her home, alone, more than she wanted to admit.

These feelings she was having around Seth were nothing but her reaction to being around a man again. A young, handsome, sexy-smelling guy who should not tempt her.

But he did.

Not because she was attracted to him. Though, she was. What woman wouldn't be? The real bottom line was a combination of things. Her having been sheltered for months combined with his good looks and their close proximity was making her supersensitive.

But it was Clark she loved. Clark she still missed.

She crawled into bed and closed her eyes, thinking about his silly laugh, how he'd loved to cook, how much he'd wanted their baby.

And all thoughts of Seth vanished.

In the middle of the night, Seth awakened to the sound of crying. Recognizing it was Crystal and he was repaying a debt, he rolled over to go back to sleep, but sleep didn't come. He put the pillow over his head. No help.

Finally, the little girl quieted, and he realized Harper must have given her a bottle or something. He fell back to sleep, woke when the alarm sounded and sneaked up the hall to the kitchen to make a cup of coffee. Their conversation the night before had been good, but they were still uncomfortable with each other. And he was still fighting that attraction. So better not to wake her.

"Good morning."

Damn. She was already up.

She wore the pale blue pajamas he'd seen the night before. They were much less revealing than things he'd seen in Vegas or Barcelona and his face should not have reddened. But it had.

She looked soft-and-cuddly sexy. Her sleepy blue eyes should have reminded him that she'd gotten up with a baby the night before. Instead they reminded him of warm, fuzzy feelings after sex.

"I just, uh, wanted a cup of coffee."

"Okay."

He neared the counter, where she sat holding the baby. The little girl looked at him.

"Hey."

Harper shot him a confused expression.

"Just, you know, saying, hey, to the kid…the baby… Crystal."

The little girl grinned.

"I think she likes you."

"Well, she terrifies me. In a good way," he quickly added. "I don't want to hurt her."

"You won't."

"Sure," he said, knowing he wouldn't ever hurt her because he wouldn't ever touch her.

He got his coffee and went back to his room, where he dressed in his typical work clothes of jeans and a halfway decent shirt. When he returned to the kitchen for his keys and wallet, Harper and the baby were gone.

Wincing, he walked back the hall and knocked on her door.

"Yes?"

"Just wanted to let you know I'm on my way to work."

"Okay."

He squeezed his eyes shut. The melodious sound of her voice drifted through him like a blast of sweet summer air. She sounded so happy and content that pride surged through him, tightening his chest. This time two days ago, she'd been facing homelessness and he'd fixed that for her.

He started up the hall and picked up his keys and wallet. What the hell was wrong with him? Helping her should feel good, but he wasn't doing this for her. He was doing it for Clark.

To pay back Clark for taking him in when he needed help.

The very fact that he kept forgetting that meant it was time to get things moving along before his emotions got any more involved.

CHAPTER THREE

THAT EVENING, SETH RETURNED a little later than he had the night before, looking like a sex god in a T-shirt that showed off his chest and shoulders and a pair of sunglasses he'd probably bought in Europe.

Harper's breathing shivered. Her muscles froze. For the next ten seconds, she was sure her heart stopped beating.

"We're going to do your résumé tonight."

"That's great." She thought of Clark, realizing how happy he'd be once she was settled, and all the feelings she'd had about Seth lessened. "But I made dinner." A thought occurred. "You haven't eaten, have you?"

"No. But the résumé probably should come first."

"Or maybe we can talk about it while we eat?" That way they wouldn't have to discuss other things. Not that she hadn't appreciated the conversation the night before. She had. It was more that it had warmed her a little too much.

"Okay."

He set the table as she brought Crystal's baby seat over and strapped it to a chair. She'd already put the pot roast and potatoes and carrots into a huge serving dish and he carried it to the table.

"Smells good." His voice sounded funny, like he had caught the scent of the food and shivered around it.

"Thanks. I learned to cook after Clark and I got married. Mrs. Petrillo watched Crystal while I checked out the little grocery store a few blocks down."

They both sat. Each of them dished up a plateful of food.

Seth took a bite and squeezed his eyes shut in ecstasy. "This is fantastic."

It had been so long since anyone had complimented her that even a simple expression of pleasure went through her like warm honey. Luckily, they had work to do.

She bounced from her chair. "I'll go get my laptop."

She raced into her bedroom and found her

computer. She turned it on, pulled up her résumé and headed to the dining area again.

When she got there, Seth was standing in front of Crystal's seat.

He glanced up at Harper. "I wasn't sure what to do. I knew you were probably okay with her sitting there. But I'm new to all this and when you were gone so long, I figured I'd better be safe rather than sorry."

Crystal grinned and he laughed. "She's really cute."

The sight of him by her little girl warmed her heart, but more than that, he was getting accustomed to her baby. Maybe growing to like her baby—

He wasn't supposed to like Crystal. Or her. She was here temporarily. They'd probably never see each other again after her short stay here. She needed to remember that.

"She's fine as long as the she's strapped in." She slid the laptop on the table. "Here's my résumé."

Seth returned to his seat. He angled the screen toward him and started reading.

After only a minute, he glanced over at her. "What kind of a job are you trying for?"

"I'd like to be somebody's assistant."

"Okay. Good. I think your qualifications should line up. But you do realize there'll be some other things like typing involved? Maybe writing reports."

"That would be fantastic. I like to work. I think I'd like a job that would challenge me."

He finished reading what she had in her résumé as he ate his roast and potatoes. After they'd cleaned the kitchen and dining area, she put the baby to bed.

When she returned to the living area, he pointed to the laptop, still on the dining room table. "Okay. We need to punch it up a bit, but we'll figure it out together. If I'm going to recommend you, I want to know what's in your résumé."

Her spirits brightened. "You're going to recommend me?"

"I saw how you worked when you lived beside me and Clark. I know you were dedicated to your clients. I know you put in long hours." He shrugged. "I'm the perfect person to recommend you."

She sat at the table in front of the laptop. He stood behind her.

Leaning in, he said, "Our first problem is that you haven't worked in five years. We have to downplay that."

The woodsy scent of his cologne floated to her. Her shoulder tingled because he had his hand on the back of her chair and every time she moved, she brushed it. Her mind tried to go blank, to enjoy the sensations, but she wouldn't let it. They had a job to do.

She turned to make a suggestion about how to get around the gap between her work experience and the current date, but when she turned, the way he leaned in put them face-to-face. So close, they could have rubbed noses.

Close enough to kiss.

Her chest froze. Where the hell had that thought come from? She did not want to kiss him. This feeling tumbling through her had to be wrong. Seth was her husband's best friend.

She started to turn away, but his eyes held hers. When she'd met him, she'd thought he had the eyes of a bad boy. Dark. Forbidding. But she once again saw the spark of wisdom or experience that she'd seen when he'd opened his condo door to her a few days before.

It was as if something had happened in the past

five years. Something that had changed him. She knew what his dad had been like. She knew his mom had been oblivious—

She blinked to break eye contact. She wasn't supposed to be curious about him.

"I, um, thought maybe we could just admit that I got married five years ago and hadn't worked since."

He pulled back. "I think you have to. The worst thing a person can do is lie on a résumé."

Surprised, she laughed. "You think *that's* the worst thing a person can do?"

He turned away. "There are definitely worse things a person can do in general. But we're talking in terms of getting a job."

"Oh. Right." She faced her laptop again, moved the cursor to the spot she needed to change and started typing. But she couldn't stop thinking about his eyes. They were not the eyes of a serial seducer. They weren't the eyes of a poet, either. They were the eyes of a cautious man.

Probably because of what had happened in his family.

Sure, he was working for them…but he'd already mentioned not being close to his mom. Whatever had caused him to run from his family must not have been resolved. Or had they swept it under the rug like a good high-society family?

Curiosity rose and knocked and knocked and knocked on her brain, begging for attention.

She ignored it.

Her wanting to know about him could be nothing more than the curiosities of a lonely woman.

They fussed with her résumé for another hour before they got it right. Then she raced off to her room and Seth was left with the scent of her shampoo lingering in his nostrils, making him crazy.

But the fact that she'd run off proved to him that he wasn't the only one feeling things. He'd seen it when she'd sat staring into his eyes. She'd covered that by being strictly professional as they tidied her résumé, but her racing off brought back all his instincts that she was every bit as attracted to him as he was to her.

Clark's widow.

That made it doubly important that he help her with her job search, so she could leave.

The baby woke him again that night and instead of pulling the pillow over his head, curiosity had him sitting up in bed. He wondered what a mother and baby did in the middle of the night. Did Harper sing to Crystal? Read to her?

He plopped back down again and pulled the pillow over his head. This was nuts. He did not like babies. They scared him. He shouldn't care about Crystal and Harper. Or even just Harper. He knew better. It was why he'd stepped aside and let Clark ask her out. Clark had been the nice guy. The guy who loved kids and wanted a family. The guy who'd found one perfect woman and would have been faithful forever.

Seth was a womanizer.

But living with Harper seemed to be making him forget the wise move he'd made when he was twenty-two. Step back. Let her be with someone who would love her correctly.

He had to get her a job and an apartment, and move out of his house…his life. Before he did something stupid.

He went to work Friday morning and called Arthur Jenkins, whose assistant was at least seven months pregnant and should be going on maternity leave. His company was small. His needs were probably few.

He talked up Harper, honestly telling Art that she didn't have office experience, but she was dedicated and a hard worker. When he mentioned that she was also funny and nice to have around, he clamped his mouth shut. Luckily, Art took everything he said in the context of an assistant and gave him a time to tell her to come for an interview Monday morning.

When Seth told her about the interview her eyes lit with joy, making him glad he hadn't canceled his date that evening. Or the one for Saturday night. Not wanting to take any chances being around her, he also left Sunday morning and didn't come back until late Sunday night.

Monday morning, he didn't knock on her door before he left for work. He texted her from his office to wish her luck on her interview and make himself seem appropriately distanced from the woman whose blue eyes could inspire poetry.

He didn't expect to hear back from her until after lunch, and relief got him through a morning of meetings. At noon, the sky was clear, the weather still warm. Feeling very good about helping Harper, he decided to accept his brother's invitation to join him for lunch at a nearby restaurant.

But as they strode toward the lobby door, Harper walked in.

He caught Jake's arm. "That's Harper."

"Harper?" His dark-haired, blue-eyed brother frowned. "Clark's wife?"

"Widow. She needed help finding a job." He craned his neck to see past the gaggle of people. "I got her an interview this morning."

Obviously surprised, Jake peered at him. "You did?"

He batted a hand. "It's nothing. But she could be here looking for me. Better go on without me."

Jake left. Seth caught up to Harper, who was standing in front of the directory. "Harper?"

She turned to him with tears in her eyes. "I didn't get it."

His heart sank, but he said, "It's your first interview. It's fine."

A tear rolled onto her cheek. "No. It's not fine. I need a job. I have a baby to support."

Her crying went through him like hot ice. He led her to the door and out onto the sidewalk, so she wouldn't stand in one place long enough for anyone to really see or hear her. Her words would blend into the noise of the city around them.

As they started up the street, she said, "Seth,

it was like a whole different world. I was even dressed wrong."

She spoke stronger now. Her tears had scared him, but the fact that she gathered herself together humbled him. He thought he was helping her, but this was really her battle. She was a good woman, a good person, in a bad situation. And she was right. In her purple skirt and simple white blouse, she wasn't dressed to impress. It was like she was hiding her light under a basket.

He glanced around and saw a small boutique up ahead. He'd frequented the store to get gifts for his mom, his sister and girlfriends. The clerks were quiet, discrete. If he took Harper inside and told the saleswomen they needed to look around, they would smile and give them some space. And he could give her some pointers on dressing for an office. Somehow in those years of being self-employed, she'd gotten the idea that office workers needed to be dowdy.

He took her arm and led her into the store.

"What are we doing?"

"You said you felt you were dressed wrong."

She looked down at her white blouse and eggplant-colored skirt. "I *was* dressed wrong. I haven't bought clothes in two years, unless you count maternity jeans."

He pointed to the left at a long rack of tops beside a rack of skirts and trousers beside a rack of sweaters beside three rows of dresses.

"See the colors?"

"Pretty." Her head tilted. "And not a dark purple skirt or blouse among them."

"Go look."

She faced him. "I can't afford to spend a bunch of cash on clothes when I'm not sure if I'll need the money for a down payment on a house."

"Maybe. But because you've never worked in an office, I think you got the wrong idea about what to wear. Just look around."

She frowned, glanced back at the racks. He could see from the way her eyes shifted that she didn't just want to fit in. She almost seemed to long to run her fingers along the fabrics, try things on, get some clothes that would ease her into her next life phase.

"I can get you an account here."

She bit her lower lip. "If I have to use my profit from selling my condo as a down payment for another condo, God knows when I'll be able to pay it off."

"Why don't you let me worry about that?"

She closed her eyes. "I can't do that."

His heart melted. He could afford to buy the whole damn store and she wouldn't let him buy her a few dresses.

"What if we get the account, but you make the payments. Probably won't be too much if you spread it out over a few months. And new clothes will give you the confidence you need on your next interview."

She licked her lips. His libido sent blood straight to the wrong part of him, as his emotions zigzagged in four different directions. He'd always had a thing for Harper. But he'd also known her as his best friend's wife. He wanted to help her. Almost *needed* to help her. But he loved her strength, her pride, her longing to make her own way and be herself.

Hell, hadn't he fought to be allowed to be himself?

"Please."

She glanced at him. "I know you're doing all this to pay back a debt to Clark. But he never felt you owed him."

"I owe him everything I am today. Which is

why I understand why you don't want to take the help."

She chuckled, then shook her head as if amazed by him. "You will let me pay the bill?"

"I'll consider forwarding that bill a sacred obligation."

"I do like that black dress back there."

He motioned for a salesgirl. "Then you should try it on."

They shopped long past Seth's lunch hour. She tried on dresses, pants, blouses, skirts, sweaters. Though Seth would have had her take it all, he let her sift through and find eight pieces she could mix and match, and three simple dresses.

The salesclerk happily tallied the price and boxed the first dress neatly. Expensively. From his days of living hand-to-mouth while at university and in his two years of working as a lowly broker for a big investment firm, he knew that little touches like a box with tissue paper made a person feel a bit better about themselves, about who they were.

He watched as the clerks tucked away the other two dresses, then the trousers, and started on the tops.

"Harper?"

The woman's voice came from behind Seth. He turned and saw a tall, black-haired woman with big blue eyes very much like Harper's.

"Mom?"

His gut almost exploded. Harper's mom wore an expensive suit, shoes that probably set her back thousands and a purse that had probably cost more. The diamond on her left hand could have blinded him. All of Harper's fears came into sharp focus for him. This was a woman who liked being rich, who thought more of money than people.

She reached out and caught Harper by the shoulders, hugged her, then kissed her cheek. "It's so lovely to see you here."

He thought the comment odd until he realized this boutique existed purely for wealthy clientele. Harper's mom didn't know her daughter was broke. She believed her daughter belonged there.

"And buying things!"

Her mother sounded thrilled, but also proud. Knowing appearances meant everything to her, he understood why she was over-the-top happy.

Harper, however, looked like a deer trapped in the headlights of an oncoming car. She opened her mouth as if trying to speak but couldn't get any words out. Her eyes drifted to the stack of clothes, almost all packed into bags and boxes now.

Unconcerned about Harper's silence, Harper's mom faced Seth. "And who is this?"

He decided to pick up the dropped ball and held his hand out to shake Harper's mom's. "I'm Seth McCallan, Mrs. Sloan."

She took his hand with a gasp. "Seth McCallan. Of course. I've seen you at a few charity functions. I'm sorry I didn't recognize you. I'm Amelia Sloan. My husband is Peter. Please call me Amelia."

He smiled. "It's nice to meet you, Amelia."

Pleasure lit Amelia Sloan's face. "What are you doing here with my Harper?"

"Just a little shopping."

The salesclerk finished boxing Harper's new clothes and casually handed the receipt to Seth.

Amelia's eyes narrowed, then widened slightly as she figured out Seth was paying for Harper's purchases.

"It's not what you think, Mom."

Amelia clucked. "And how would you know what I think?"

While the women seemed to be on the same

page, Seth needed a minute to process why Harper was struggling. Drowning really. Here was the very person Harper wanted to keep her situation from, standing in front of them, seeing someone buying clothes for her daughter. She didn't know Harper was broke or that she intended to pay Seth for the purchases. And he realized explaining that might make things worse. Amelia would ask why Harper had to have someone else pay for her clothes, everything Harper was trying to hide would come tumbling out and the thing he'd spent a week of torture to avoid would happen.

Amelia Sloan would blame Clark.

There was only one way to fix this...

"We're dating."

The words came out of Seth's mouth in a rush, as if the quicker he said it, the quicker Amelia would stop going down a road that Harper didn't want her traveling.

But where Amelia's face glowed with happy surprise, Harper's mouth fell open.

Her reaction would have ruined everything if Seth hadn't thought to step closer and put his arm around her waist.

Amelia all but melted with joy. "You didn't

want me to know you were dating one of the most eligible men in Manhattan? Harper! That's ridiculous."

"No, it's not. Because we're not—"

Seth squeezed her waist. "We're not serious. Just started seeing each other," he said, trying to mitigate the lie.

Amelia's eyes narrowed. "And you thought my Harper didn't dress well enough for your rarefied world?"

"No!" Seth assured her, scrambling for what to say. "She said she liked something in the window." Oh, crap. Another lie. "And I wanted to buy it for her." He *had* wanted to buy her clothes. "Because it pleases me to give her things." That, too, was the truth. Remembering the joyful expression on Harper's face when the clothes she loved had looked so good on her, he'd give away half his trust fund to see that look on her face again.

"Well, that's sweet." Amelia hugged her daughter. "I'd love to get coffee and chat, but I have something this afternoon. Why don't you and Seth bring the baby over some night."

"I'm sorry. We probably can't. We're kind of busy, too," Seth explained before Harper could answer. This might not be the perfect lie, but it would hold long enough to get Harper settled in a job and a house. Once they left the store and were away from her mom, he could tell her that. "But I'll have my assistant call yours tomorrow and they can set something up like dinner."

"That would be lovely," Amelia said, her eyes glowing.

Seth quickly grabbed the packages and herded Harper toward the door. "We'll see you then."

Amelia waved.

Harper reminded stonily quiet.

When they stepped out onto the street, he wasn't surprised that she pivoted on him. "You have no idea what you've done."

"I got you out of the store without having to admit anything to your mom."

"Yeah, but now she'll start snooping."

"Into what?" He laughed. "She can call the tabloids, if she wants, looking for times we went out, places we've gone. But she's not going to find anything."

"And she'll get suspicious."

"So what?"

"You are such a babe in the woods. I'm either

going to have to come clean with her, and soon, or we're going to have to keep up this charade."

"Would it be such a big deal to keep it up?"

She cast him a long look. "You can't date anyone while you're pretending to be dating me."

"I feel uncomfortable leaving you alone at night, anyway." He sighed. He hated lying. His father had been the consummate liar. He'd used lies to control, manipulate, humiliate, belittle and bully everyone from his employees to his own children. If there was one thing Seth had vowed never to do, it was lie.

But this was a worthy cause, an unusual situation. Harper, a widow with a baby, needed time to get herself settled before she told her mom she was broke and it was Clark's fault.

Plus, her mom hadn't appeared on the radar of Seth's life before this. He didn't think she'd start now. Unlike his father's master manipulation lies, this little charade wouldn't hurt anyone.

"Needing to get out of this mess will step up your job search a bit and we might have to start looking for houses before you have a job…but I think I did what I had to do."

"You're willing to pretend to be my boyfriend for at least the next *four weeks*?"

The ramifications of that rained down on him. No breakfasts, lunches or dinners with any women except colleagues…and no sex.

She shook her head. "That's a long time."

Yeah, that was sinking in and not pleasantly.

"And my mother is relentless. You're a catch. She's going to want me to keep you."

That, thank God, made him laugh. "My reputation will save us. When we break up no one will be surprised."

"Oh, really?"

"Yes. You're taking this all too seriously. It's a few weeks. What can she possibly do in a few weeks?"

CHAPTER FOUR

WHAT CAN SHE do in a few weeks?

Harper groaned. "You'd be surprised. So, we do have to step up the job search and the apartment hunt."

"I already said that."

She glanced at the armful of boxes he carried and the bags she had in her hand. "I'm going to need a cab."

"No. Jake's car is just up the street." Juggling the boxes, he pulled out his phone, hit a few buttons and said, "Does Jake need you today?" He listened, then smiled. "Good. I have a friend who only has to go a few blocks, but she's been shopping and has bags." A pause. "Okay. We're not even a block up the street from the office. You'll see us on the sidewalk."

He disconnected the call. "He'll check in with Jake and be here in two minutes. I'll wait with you." He displayed the boxes. "Because I don't think you can handle all these."

They stood in silence until the limo pulled up. The trunk popped. The driver jumped out and took the packages from Harper, tucking them into the trunk. Seth handed him the boxes he held, and he stowed them away before returning to open the passenger door of the limo.

She turned to say thanks to Seth, but saw her mom coming out of the boutique—just in time to see her standing in front of a McCallan limo.

"Don't look now but my mom is behind you."

Seth's eyebrows drew together. "She is?"

"I told you, her curiosity knows no bounds."

"She's looking?"

"Of course, she's looking!"

"Then we'll just have to make this realistic." He leaned in and placed a soft kiss on her lips. The movement was smooth, a light brush across her mouth, but it rained tingles down to her toes. Her breath hitched, caught in her chest and froze.

She thought he'd pull away. He didn't. She told herself she should move back, but she couldn't. All those questions about him rose up in her, but so did the sweet sensations of being attracted to someone. Of feeling like a woman.

He took a step closer. She took a step toward him. His arms circled her waist. Her hands went to his shoulders. The kiss deepened. The press of his lips became a crush. Arousal blossomed in her belly, scrambled her pulse, shattered her concentration.

When he moved his mouth, she opened hers for him—

And common sense returned.

Not only was her mother watching, but Harper was also kissing Clark's best friend…and a womanizer. Even if he wasn't Clark's best friend, he was all wrong for her. And she missed Clark. She didn't want another man. Not yet. She didn't want to lose Clark's memory…to forget him.

She jerked back. Not risking another glance into those dark eyes of his, she took the few steps from the sidewalk to the limo. As casually as possible, she said, "I'll see you at home."

She slid into the limo. She didn't wait to see Seth's reaction, didn't peer at the boutique door to see if her mom was still watching. There was no need. The damage had been done. Not only did her mom think she was dating one of the wealthiest men in Manhattan, but that man had also kissed her. Greedily. Hungrily.

She could close her eyes and remember the kiss. Every movement of his mouth.

The limo sped off and she covered her face with her hands. She didn't know which was worse—her mom thinking she was dating a catch or liking the kiss of a man she shouldn't be kissing. Clark might be gone, but he wasn't forgotten. She'd adored him. She didn't want to replace him.

She wasn't even ready to *think about* replacing him.

She wasn't even ready to think about *liking* someone.

After flubbing her interview that morning, she'd thought her situation couldn't get any worse, and in the blink of an eye—or the brush of some lips—it had worsened exponentially.

Because worse than the longing that had sprung up inside her, worse than the kiss, worse than her mom thinking she and Seth were dating, was a deep sadness, a quiet reminder whispered from the depths of her soul that Clark was gone.

Seth stood watching the limo drive off. He'd kissed a lot of women in his lifetime but, somehow, he'd always known kissing Harper would be different. Every cell in his body had awakened. His blood had electrified. His mind shot back eight years, to when he should have asked her out—instead of stepping away so Clark could ask her out. Back to when he'd still believed in miracles, in magic, and he remembered his yearning to make her his.

He turned to walk to his building. Knowing her mom was watching, he kept his expression neutral. He didn't smile or frown or grimace until he was behind the closed door of his office, then he had to hold back a howl of misery. *He could not have that woman.* He was a serial dater. No. He wasn't even that nice. He was a one-night-stand guy. Harper was a woman with a child. *A widow.* She needed security. He did not get involved with women like her because he didn't want to hurt anyone. His definition of making a woman "his" now was very different than what it had been eight years ago.

He could not kiss her again.

But he wanted to.

And that's what made him nuts. Until he'd kissed her he'd been curious. And, yeah, maybe a little needy for it. But he'd been smart enough to ignore the urge. Now that he knew how great kissing her was, he would think of that kiss every time he looked at her.

But he would also know he couldn't kiss her again.

And that would make him even more nuts.

He sat in his chair and threw himself into his projects as if his life depended on it. Around two, his stomach growled. He hadn't had lunch. He got a snack cake from the vending machine in the employee lounge and went back to work.

He should have left at six. He waited until seven. But he couldn't stay any longer. If he did, Harper would wonder why and probably realize a kiss that was supposed to be a show for her mom had been a little too real for him.

Of course, she had kissed him back.

Cursing himself for reminding himself of that, he rode the elevator up to his floor, then ambled down the hall. Using his key, he opened the door and stepped inside.

"I'm home."

He almost cursed again. He sounded like a husband.

"We're in the kitchen."

He walked into the main area and found Harper at the island, sitting on a stool, feeding Crystal a bottle.

The silence in the room was so thick, he

scrambled for something to say. Anything to get them over the awkwardness. "So, she drinks milk?"

Harper glanced over at him. Probably confused by the stupid question. Still, she answered it. "She drinks formula."

"Formula" sounded like something made in a laboratory. Sympathy for the kid filled him. Glad to forget his misery over kissing Harper, he sat on the stool beside them.

"She seems to like it."

"Do you think I'd feed her something she didn't like?"

After a few seconds, the bottle was empty. Harper rose and patted the little girl's back until she burped like a sailor.

She laughed. "Okay. That's enough for now."

She buckled Crystal into the baby carrier, which she fastened to one of the tufted chairs around the dining room table.

"I made dinner."

He wished with all his might that he could get out of eating with her, but his stomach growled. "What'd you make?"

"I was going to make spaghetti, but I think Mrs. P. plans to make that for you next week."

His mouth watered. Mrs. P. was a wonderful person to have for a neighbor. Which reminded him—

"How did she do babysitting while you were at your interview this morning?"

"She loved having someone to watch her morning soap operas with." Harper airily moved into the kitchen, over to the oven, and pulled out a casserole. "She told me that she'd be happy to keep Crystal anytime I have an interview or a condo to look at."

"That's good."

"She also loved the clothes we picked out." She lifted the casserole to the countertop, pausing for a second before she turned to Seth. "I'm sorry about my mom."

He reached for his mail to give himself something to look at other than her apologetic blue eyes. "It's fine."

"No. It's not fine. She's a snob and a gossip and just plain hard to get along with."

"I already told you my dad wasn't exactly a prince. In fact, he was so bad he makes your mom look good."

Her quick laugh told him he'd sufficiently gotten her past her embarrassment about her mom.

Now, if she'd just not say anything about—

"I'm also sorry you had to kiss me."

Just the mention of it turned him on again, while Harper still appeared apologetic. Only apologetic. Not breathless. Not curious. The kiss might as well have not happened.

A little annoyed, a little insulted, he tossed the mail on the counter. "It's not like I had to scoop up dog poop. Besides, I seem to remember the kiss was my idea."

And that she'd participated. She hadn't stayed still. It hadn't been like kissing a rock.

"Okay. Maybe instead of apologizing I should say thanks."

She should. She really should because he was suffering the torment of the damned and she'd gotten away from her mom without having to explain that she was broke.

He was a prince, a saint, to have helped her.

Especially since every time they discussed her mom, he thought of his dad. The humiliation. The fact that things weren't right with his own mom and would never really be right.

His phone rang. He glanced at caller ID and saw it was a female friend who visited New York only a few times a year. Glad for the interruption of his thoughts, he answered it. "Marlene! How are you?"

He drifted toward the sofa for privacy, knowing this was exactly what he needed. The reminder that he was a *happy* serial-one-night-stand guy. Not a knight who rescued nice women. Not a guy who thought too much about his past with an abusive father and a mom who turned a blind eye.

"I'm in town. Want to get a drink?"

"I'd love a drink." He needed a drink. "Where and what time?"

"I'm staying at the Waldorf. There's a lovely club just down the street."

"I'll meet you there in a few minutes."

He disconnected the call and headed for the door. "Sorry, but that was an old friend. I'm meeting her for drinks."

One of her eyebrows rose. He was absolutely positive she was going to remind him he wasn't allowed to date, so he added, "Seriously. She's just a friend. A business associate. If I pay, I can write this off as an expense."

"Oh. Okay."

He'd never heard two words said with such relief and that compounded the I'm-an-idiot feelings currently bubbling through him like stew in a big, black witch's pot.

All she was worried about was keeping the charade intact. While he was mad at himself for kissing Clark's wife, thinking thoughts about his parents that he'd believed he'd left behind when his dad died, and worried about his attraction to a nice woman when he was so unreliable, she was only worried about fooling her mom.

Not that he blamed her. He understood how hard it was to try to please an unpleasable parent.

"Have a nice time."

"I will." He headed out to meet Marlene.

He left for work the next morning after not much more than a few grunts in Harper's direction. Respectful of his mood, Harper didn't say anything, either. That kiss by the limo the day before had ruined the complicated but civil relationship they were developing. She knew that was why he'd eagerly accepted the chance to get out of the condo the night before. And why she'd been so glad he had.

The kiss had been amazing. Because of Clark, she'd talked herself out of making a big deal out of it. But it wasn't easy. Seth was an experienced kisser. She remembered every brush of his lips. Every sweep of his tongue. When she least expected it, she'd remember it, and had to admit, she'd liked it.

But maybe Seth hadn't. In fact, his edginess the night before and grumpiness that morning might be a sign he *regretted* kissing her. Not a sign that he'd liked it.

She smacked the side of her own head, hoping to knock some sense into herself. It was crazy, stupid, to think about it. The damn kiss had only been part of a charade. Plus, she had bigger problems that should be occupying her mind and her time. Like a job and a place to live.

While Crystal slept, she brought her laptop to the kitchen island and searched for jobs online, keeping her cell phone beside her with the baby-monitor app opened.

An hour into her fruitless search, her phone rang. The sound echoed through the quiet condo and almost made her jump out of her skin.

Seeing her mom's picture pop up on the screen, she grimaced. She'd want the juicy details about Seth. Harper was either going to have to continue the lie or tell the truth…which would open the can of worms Harper had kept tightly closed for the past year.

She took a breath. Blew it out slowly. Then answered. "Hey, Mom."

"Good morning, sweetie. How's Crystal today?"

"The same as always." She slid off the stool and paced into the area with the sofa and television, her feet drifting along the soft shag of the white area rug on the rustic brown hardwood floor.

"Has she said 'Nana' yet?"

"No. She hasn't even said 'Mom.' Right now, we're working on getting her to say 'goo.'"

"She'll say it. Then 'Mom' will follow and pretty soon she'll be saying 'Nana,'" her mother said enthusiastically. "I'm calling because I haven't heard from Seth's people yet."

Harper squeezed her eyes shut, still undecided about what to say. Did she admit that she and Seth weren't dating? Did she say he was helping her find a job? Did she mention that he was letting her live with him—because she was nearly broke? And if she did, how would she handle her mom's anger?

She stalled. "It hasn't even been twenty-four hours."

"I know. But when a man like Seth is dating a classy woman like you, he's Johnny on the spot with things like dinner invitations."

She glanced down at her worn jeans and the shirt that had stretched out from too many washings. She was hardly classy.

But this was her opening to end the charade. She had to take it. She didn't like the lie—or Seth's regret. "Mom, this thing with me and Seth—"

"I know. You're not making a big deal out of it. In fact, you're probably brooding because of Clark, but it's time, Harper."

The easy way her mother dismissed Clark set her nerve endings on fire. "Time for what, Mom?"

"To let go. To date. To think about marrying again."

Oh, Lord. She already had them married? "Mom, Seth is thirty-one and he's never married—"

"Because he's particular. Many wealthy men wait until their thirties to marry, even their forties, because they have enough female attention that they don't need to marry the wrong woman.

Though some do. Look at George Clooney. He waited until his fifties to settle down for good."

Harper frowned at her phone. Her mother certainly knew how to whitewash things she wanted cleaned and sanitized.

"That's one way of looking at it. The other is that they like dating, don't want a commitment, don't want kids."

Her heart pinged when she remembered Seth telling her he was afraid of kids. Even if that kiss had caused her to swoon, this was reality. Seth didn't like kids. She had a child. There would be nothing between them.

Her mind cleared. And while it was clear, she wanted it to stay clear. It was time to tell her mother the truth.

"Mom, what you saw yesterday—"

"Was adorable. Stop talking yourself out of liking Seth because you think he's is too good for you. Don't be angry, honey, but I know that's why you married Clark. Lack of self-confidence."

Anger burst in Harper's chest. "Mom, Clark was a gorgeous blond. He could have had his pick of women. I was lucky he chose me."

"You were young and thinking with your hormones. But we don't have to worry about that with Seth. He's gorgeous *and* has money. No. Not just money—a pedigree. He is someone."

"He's someone, all right. Probably a better person than you think he is." She opened her mouth to explain Seth was helping her out of her bad situation, but the words stuck in her throat. With the way this conversation was going, if Harper told her mother that she needed Seth's help because Clark had left her broke, her mom would explode. The only way *that* discussion went smoothly would be if Harper had a job and a place to stay when she told her parents that she'd had to sell the investment firm and her condo.

She needed time. Seth's lie bought her time.

"You know what, Mom? I think dinner with you and Dad is too soon."

After a short pause, her mom said, "Too soon?"

"We're barely dating." At least that wasn't a lie. "I think we just need to be on our own for a while."

Her mom sighed. "I get it."

Surprised that she'd given up so easily, Harper said, "You do?"

"Sure. Nobody starts out dating by introducing a guy to her parents. It was a fluke that we ran into each other, but that doesn't mean we

can push the schedule along and ruin things."
Her mom took a long breath. "But your father
and I also can't ignore you, if we see you around
town."

Relief and disbelief of her luck fluttered
through her. "You won't see us."

Her mom laughed. "You're so sure of that?
Your dad and I eat out five times a week. We
go to parties. Now that you're with a man in our
league, you're bound to run into us."

*No, they wouldn't. Because she and Seth would
never go anywhere.*

Harper's chest loosened. Her blood began to
flow again. She desperately needed the next few
weeks to get her life in order. If it meant her
mom had to think she was dating Manhattan's
most eligible bachelor...so be it.

"Thanks, Mom."

"You're welcome." She paused. "You could
still come by with the baby some afternoon when
Seth is working."

"I have a few things I have to straighten out."

Her mom's voice soured. "Clark's estate still
not settled?"

"Something like that." She winced, thinking of
the whirlwind job search and house hunting in

her near future and oh, so glad she hadn't ended the lie. "But as soon as I'm free, Crystal and I will be over."

"Good. I love you," her mom said in a sing-song voice.

Harper said, "I love you, too."

She disconnected the call, wishing she could mean it. She knew her mom's intentions were good. But even as Amelia Sloan happily chatted about Seth, she'd subtly bad-mouthed Clark. When Harper finally told her mom that she'd lost Clark's investment firm because it was barely worth what he'd owed on it and sold the condo because Clark had mortgaged that, too, she had to have everything sorted or Amelia would have the kind of tirade about Clark that broke Harper's heart.

Seth had been correct. The lie really would hold for a few weeks. It had, too.

A little after six, Seth arrived home and Harper didn't waste a second. He'd run out of the apartment the night before and that morning because things were tense between them. She could fix that.

"My mom called this morning."

His expression shifted from neutral to cautious. "I forgot to have someone phone her about dinner."

"It's fine. I told her we had just started dating and needed a few weeks 'on our own' and she agreed."

His face contorted. "What does that mean?"

"It means she won't be calling or dropping by. We're fine."

He studied her for a few seconds. "I thought you said she was a meddler."

"She is. She's a smart one. She agreed to the pull-back to make sure she didn't ruin things before they start. But the bottom line is she's giving us a few weeks. Which means I can find a job, find a house, move out…and then tell her we broke up. Which will horrify her as much as Clark putting us in debt. I'll take most of the heat for her anger." She shrugged. "In a way, this charade is perfect."

Seth stared at Harper. The way she always deflected bad things away from Clark and to herself amazed him. But this time, it also made him a little angry with Clark that he'd put Harper in this position. Still, he'd never tell Harper that.

And all things considered, he'd rather have their attention on her mom, than that kiss.

"So, you think she's going to let us alone?"

"Yes. We should be fine. As long as we don't go out."

The house phone rang. He walked to the island where it sat. Seeing the caller was Rick, another doorman, he answered. "What's up, Rick?"

"Your mother is here." There was a knock on his door. "I already sent her up."

Confusion made him frown, but he said, "Okay. That's fine."

He turned to Harper. "That knock at the door is *my* mother."

"Oh! Should I hide?"

The door opened before he could answer. He'd forgotten he'd given his mom a key in case of emergencies. Maureen McCallan looked past Seth and to Harper. She took in her torn jeans and bare feet.

"So, it's true. You *are* living with Harper Hargraves."

"It's not what you think."

"Really? Her mom bragged about it to everybody at the ladies who lunch meeting this afternoon."

He started to say they weren't living together in the conventional sense of the word, but then he'd have to explain the charade. If he told his mom the truth and his mom told someone, who told someone, who told Harper's mom, it would ruin everything.

He stuck to the lie. "It's more like we're dating."

"So, Harper's just here for dinner?" She sniffed the air. "You made French toast casserole?" She faced Seth. "You don't cook that well, Seth."

"I made it, Mrs. McCallan."

His mom gave Harper another quick once-over. "If you're dating my son, you can call me Maureen."

Harper swallowed hard and caught Seth's gaze. He hadn't believed her when she'd warned him the lie could cause trouble. Still, it was only for a few weeks and it wasn't like he was hurting a perfect mother/son relationship.

Maureen headed for the door. "Well, I have plans for tonight and don't want to interrupt your dinner. We'll catch up at the opening for the gallery on Saturday."

So much for not being seen in public. The gallery—Hot Art—was only reopening after his family had bankrolled renovations. He couldn't miss it. And now he couldn't go without Harper.

"Yes. We'll see you then."

CHAPTER FIVE

HARPER AND CLARK had gone to fund-raisers at various art galleries, and she knew most women wore cocktail dresses.

Shopping with Seth, she hadn't bought a cocktail dress, but she had bought a simple black sheath that she could dress up with pearls. The outfit was simple and elegant. She looked like the lady her mom wanted her to be.

Little black dress.

Dating Manhattan's most eligible bachelor.

Forgetting Clark.

Except she wasn't forgetting Clark. She and Seth weren't really dating. After her mom's promise to stay out of things, this ruse was supposed to be simple, easy, because they weren't really going out in public. Then his mom had showed up and now they were hip-deep in a lie.

She stepped out of her bedroom and Mrs. P. gasped. "Oh, you look so lovely. Old-style classy."

Harper laughed. "Did you just call me old?"

Wearing a tux, Seth came from behind Mrs. P.

He looked *amazing*. His long, limber body wore a tux with the elegant grace of a man accustomed to the fine things in life. But his face bore the oddest expression. His eyes had widened. His eyebrows had raised.

"She said you looked good. And you do."

"You don't need to be so surprised."

"I'm not. I'm just accustomed to seeing you in jeans."

Ragged jeans and worn T-shirts. Her chin lifted. She might not be allowed to be attracted to him, but that didn't mean she didn't have any pride. "You saw me in cocktail dresses plenty of times when Clark and I went to these functions."

"Yeah, but you were married then—and to my best friend. I never really looked at you."

Mrs. P. chortled. "You're digging yourself farther down, Seth. Quit while you're ahead."

"Baby's already in bed for the night," Harper told Mrs. P., handing her a short list of instructions.

Mrs. P. glanced at the paper. "If she'll probably sleep the whole time you're gone, why do I need these?"

"In case she wakes up."

"Ah."

Seth walked to the island and grabbed his keys. "Let's get this show on the road."

When his condo door closed behind them, she caught his arm to stop him. "I'm sorry."

"For?"

"This whole charade is turning into a big mess." She felt like a burden. A chore. A weird something attached to his life that he would soon grow to hate. And the thought that he'd end up hating her tightened her chest and made her wish she'd never asked him for help.

"It's not a big mess. It's a gallery opening. We'll show up, have a few drinks and be back in time for Mrs. P. to catch her eleven-thirty movie."

He said it so easily that Harper's chest loosened. "You're okay with this?"

"I started it, remember? It's a couple of weeks out of my life. We're fine."

They rode the elevator to the basement garage in silence, then stepped out into rows of luxury cars. She spotted her Explorer quickly, if only because it was the one car valued at less than a hundred thousand dollars.

Which meant the Ferrari beside it was Seth's. "Wow."

He opened the door for her. "You like?"

"I love it." When Seth walked around to the driver's side and slid in beside her, she said, "Clark wanted one of these but thought the SUV was more practical."

"It probably was."

"Yeah, but it wasn't a convertible."

He laughed and started the car. "I'm guessing that means you want the top down."

"Oh, yeah." She couldn't deny it. She'd had a convertible when she was sixteen and had loved it. When she'd left home, left her parents' wealth and hypocrisy behind, it was the only thing she'd missed.

He pushed a button and the roof lowered, then he shifted gears and sent them roaring out of the parking garage.

The feeling of the wind in her hair made her laugh out loud. She'd been so concerned about involving Seth, getting a job and finding a condo that she hadn't had a second of peace. And this— the wind, the night air, forgetting her responsibilities for a few hours—was just what she needed.

"I forgot how this messes up hair," he said,

shouting over the noise of the air circulating around them.

"I don't care," she said, and meant it. "Mine's so short, I can pull my fingers through it and get it in shape again."

"Good!" He hit the gas and sent the car speeding up the street.

The air felt fantastic. Freeing. Thanks to Mrs. P. and the need to shop for groceries, she'd had a few times away from the baby, but they hadn't felt like this. Like she was allowed to be herself. Not just a mom, not a cook, not someone scrambling for a job and maybe a place to live, but herself. Her old self.

She turned and yelled, "This is fabulous."

"I know. I sometimes drive to Jersey just for the hell of it."

She sucked in more air, let it wash over her like a spring rain renewing the world. But in the blink of an eye, they pulled up to the valet in front of the gallery. He opened Harper's door and helped her out of the low sports car as Seth got out on his side. Seth tossed him the keys, then took Harper's arm.

"Ready?"

She turned and smiled at him. "Yes."

* * *

Everything male in Seth awoke. She made the simple black dress and pearls stunning with her pale skin and big blue eyes. But her pleasure during their ride over with the top down had filled him with joy. He hated that this charade seemed to trouble her, and for one darn night he wished she could forget it all and have a good time. In fact, maybe that should be his mission. Not to romance her or steer clear of her for fear of feelings, but to show her a good time. Just because she was a friend.

The doorman didn't check the list for Seth's name. Everyone knew Seth was a McCallan. He opened the door, and Seth ushered Harper inside. As the door closed, the sounds of the city were immediately replaced by the noise of conversations rising to the high ceiling of the gallery and echoing back.

Harper said, "Wow. They've remodeled this place since the last time I was here. It's gorgeous."

She was gorgeous with her windblown spiky hair and her sheath outlining her trim figure. And for the first time in what felt like forever, he wanted to show off his date.

Who wasn't really a date.

But why not?

Most of the world thought they were dating anyway.

And he'd already decided he wanted her to have a good time. Maybe they could both enjoy this.

His brother, Jake, and wife, Avery, approached them. Avery's red hair and big green eyes paired with Jake's dark hair and blue eyes made them the perfect all-American couple.

Jake said, "Harper! It is nice to see you out and about again."

Harper sucked in a breath. "Thank you."

She was obviously nervous, and Seth prayed Jake wouldn't say something about Clark. The guy had been gone a year. Harper was showing signs of really getting beyond his death. If Jake said something now—

"This is my wife, Avery." Jake faced her. "Avery, this is Harper Hargraves. She's an old friend of Seth's."

Avery smiled and shook Harper's hand. She exchanged a quick look with Jake before she answered, "I remember."

But that was all she said. She didn't mention

that she was with Jake when he got word Clark had been killed in an accident. She didn't say she'd been part of the search for Seth when he'd gone missing that night, or that they'd found him drunk and had to drive him home.

Seth hid a sigh of relief. Avery could have said any one of a million things. But his well-bred brother and his beautiful wife left out the sad details and welcomed Harper.

Jake said, "What do you think of the renovations?"

Harper glanced around. "The place is lovely."

"We wanted more space for displays, especially bigger pieces of art," Avery explained. "So, when the gallery came to us for help, we had it designed to fit almost anything."

"It's beautiful."

"Avery is the benevolent one," Jake said with a laugh. "I'd have given them the money and said have at it. She actually worked with the designers and architects."

Seth laughed at that. His brother was right about Avery being benevolent, but Avery also had changed Jake, made him kinder and gentler. Though it would be a cold frosty day in hell before Seth told his older brother that.

"Hey, everybody." Seth and Jake's sister joined the group.

"Sabrina," Seth said. "You're probably too young to remember Harper, Clark Hargrave's wife."

Sabrina extended her hand to shake Harper's. "Of course, I remember. I'm only three years younger than you are, Seth."

Harper said, "How are you, Sabrina?"

She looked expensively elegant in her sparkly blue dress, which matched her blue eyes and brought out the best in her blond hair. "Overworked. Underappreciated."

Harper laughed, and Seth swallowed another sigh of relief. He shouldn't care if his brother and sister liked Harper, but he did. He blamed that on his fear that one of them would say something about Clark's death and ruin Harper's evening, but so far no one had. Which was odd. He'd have at least expected his brother to razz him about bringing a date.

He turned to his sister. "That's what you get for working for a charity."

Sabrina's chin lifted. "We're not a charity. Clients pay what they can for our services."

Seth addressed Harper. "Sabrina runs an organization that helps startup companies."

"That's interesting!"

"It's fabulous," Sabrina said. "People come to me with their ideas and I help them bring them to life."

Harper sighed with envy. "You wouldn't happen to need an assistant, would you?"

Seth quickly intervened. "Even if she does, she can't afford you. You need a job that pays you a fairly substantial amount of money."

Sabrina looked crushed. "Too bad."

Avery said, "I can keep my ear to the ground."

"I'd appreciate that." Harper shifted her purse from one hand to the other and Seth realized that her nails were painted. The little detail, another confirmation that she'd looked forward to this event, reinforced his vow that he would help her have a good time.

Which probably meant he should get her away from his family.

"Why don't we get a drink?" Seth said.

"Better yet," Jake said, "why don't you and I go and get drinks for the ladies?"

There was no way out of that without explaining he wanted to get Harper away from his family. He headed toward the bar.

Jake followed him. "I thought you were just helping her find a job? Now you and Harper are dating?"

He shrugged. "So?"

"So? Seth? She isn't just Clark's wife. You brought her somewhere she'd have to meet family. Are you serious about her?"

"It's not like that. We're together a lot because of updating her résumé, that kind of thing. Dating just evolved from that."

"Oh...that explains why you look so chummy."

He walked up to the bar, absently ordered a Scotch. "Chummy?" He laughed, suddenly seeing the humor in stringing this out and teasing his brother. "What the hell does chummy look like?"

Jake shrugged. "You know. Exchanging glances because you share information. That kind of thing."

"You sound like an old woman."

"No. I sound like a confused brother. During everything we went through with Dad, we've told each other everything. Now you show up with Clark Hargraves's widow and you don't think I'll be curious?"

For a split second, the ruse didn't seem so funny. He and Jake had been bound by a mutual need to get out of a bad situation. He could understand his brother would be curious as to why he'd kept something so big from him.

"Jake, I like Harper." He did. No lie there. "But she's Clark's widow. She needs help. I'm helping her."

"And dating."

"And dating. But neither one of us expects anything to come of it."

Jake laughed. "You are such a babe in the woods. That's exactly how love hits. When you least expect it."

"I'm fine."

"You think so but what seems like an innocent connection combines with sexual attraction, before you know it you're hooked."

The truth of that sank into his bones like a warning that had been right in front of him, but he'd kept missing. He'd always been attracted to Harper, and now they were sharing a condo. He was helping her. She was even cooking for him.

And tonight, he'd wanted to show her a good time…

"I think I'm smart enough to keep my wits about me."

"Too bad."

Just when he thought he had a handle on the conversation, his brother threw him another curveball. "Too bad?"

"Yes. She's nice." Jake's gaze drifted to Harper and Avery and Sabrina. "And Avery likes her. No better litmus test than that." Jake suddenly grinned. "Except Mom." Jake laughed. "Oh, it's going to be fun watching you explain this to Mom."

"She's already been to the house. She heard the rumor that we were dating, and she came by."

"Well, damn. I was kind of looking forward to the show."

"There is no show."

Or at least he hoped there wouldn't be. They hadn't yet run into his mom. But now that Jake had mentioned it, he could be prepared for that, too.

Seth took a glass of champagne from a passing waiter then retrieved the Scotch he'd ordered at the bar. Jake did the same. When they returned to Avery, Harper and Sabrina, the three women were laughing.

Seth's breath stalled in his chest. He hadn't seen her laugh so deeply, so happily, since before Clark's death. But more than that, there was no one as beautiful as Harper when she laughed.

And suddenly he saw what Jake had seen. All those old feelings he had about Harper kept bubbling up when he least expected. And when they did, he froze or gazed at her, probably with adoring eyes.

Rather than panic, he decided that might be good. They were supposed to be dating. He could use these feelings, these instincts and impulses, while they were here, among the people they were trying to fool, and be warned of them when he and Harper were alone.

He rejoined the group as they subtly moved a little farther into the cluster of potential donors to the charity hosting the event. Before he took his final step in the move, Harper laid her hand on his upper arm and held him back.

"Your family put millions of dollars into the renovations for this gallery?"

"My mother enjoys being a patron of the arts." He grimaced. "We're actually silent partners."

The way her eyes brightened told him that pleased her. "Oh."

"We don't let a lot of the work we do, the things we own, get out to the general public." He paused, then caught her gaze. She trusted him with all her secrets. He could certainly trust her with one of his. "Sabrina paints. You'll find a lot of her work here under the name Sally Mc-Millen."

"You guys didn't open this gallery for her, did you?"

He laughed. "No. The gallery discovered her but her first showing was a disaster. People bought her art seeking favors from my father or just wanting to have something done by a Mc-Callan. She was embarrassed and upset. Wondered if people liked her work at all."

"I can understand that."

"Now her work is shown as Sally McMillen. She knows that the people who buy it like it for what it is. And she has a good job that acts as a cover for people."

Harper's gaze strayed to Sabrina. "She's so lucky to be talented."

"You're talented."

She turned back to him. "Not hardly."

"You cook. You care for a baby. Plus, I remember you having a booming business when we were at university. You made enough money for rent and tuition. While Clark, Ziggy and I had to live together, you could afford your own place."

She smiled sheepishly. "I was pretty good."

"You were amazing."

Their gazes caught and held. Everything Jake had said about Harper came tumbling back. He suddenly wondered what it would be like if they could have something. If *he* could do this. Fall in love. Create a life—

That was a lot to wish for from a guy who'd spent his thirty-one years knowing he'd never get married, never even get serious about a woman.

He directed Harper to catch up to Jake, Avery and Sabrina by putting his hand on her waist. One of Jake's eyebrows rose and Seth shook his head. Some days he swore his brother liked acting like a kid. Teasing him about a girl.

But not just any girl—the girl he would have let himself love if he hadn't been so scarred from his parents' marriage.

The conversation with his siblings and sister-in-law continued with everyone giving Harper tips on what skills she would need to be a good assistant. Harper matched them to things she had done as a dog-walker, gift-buyer and party-planner when she owned her own company.

Sabrina grew thoughtful. "You know, if you had a few months to get this business up and running, I might suggest that rather than find a job, you just pick up where you left off with your own business."

"I have a three-month-old. I can't leave at odd hours of the day or night to walk dogs."

"No," Sabrina said, still thoughtful. "But you could hire college kids to do that work."

"Oh! That sounds interesting."

Seth quickly intervened. "But you can't be newly self-employed and get a loan for a house or condo or even get yourself approved to rent something. You have to have a job."

All eyes turned to Seth. Everybody frowned.

"We're not just dating." He started seeing what Jake had been warning him about. He was dating a woman. Living with her. Being seen in public with her. Fooling his family for her. Because he liked her. He'd *always* liked her. "She came to me for help and advice and if that means I have to be the voice of reason, then so be it."

"Hello, darling."

Everyone turned at the sound of Amelia Sloan's voice. As Harper faced her mom, Amelia took her by the shoulders and pulled her in for a hug. "I told you we'd be running into each other."

She motioned to her right. "Seth, this is my husband, Harper's dad, Peter."

Peter shook Seth's hand. A tall brute of a man, he wore his tux with as much grace and elegance as Amelia wore her slim pink dress.

Seth said, "It's nice to meet you."

Pete's eyes glowed. "It's great to meet you, too." He didn't say anything about Seth and Harper being an item. Amelia must have threatened him with death if he ruined this for Harper. But he didn't have to. His happiness over their dating was there in his eyes.

Everything sunk in a little more for Seth. This might be a charade to fool Harper's mom, but by the next morning most of the city of New York would believe he and Harper were an item. His family, his friends and the people he did business with would know he was dating his best friend's widow.

Because he was. That was the bottom line. What started out as fake was feeling very real. And maybe that wasn't bad. He'd always liked her. He'd always wanted to woo her. Tonight, he'd wanted to show her a good time, not for the charade but because he liked her.

He *liked* her.

Maybe this was his chance.

Older, wiser, maybe he could have something with her?

"Peter, Amelia, this is Jake and Avery, my brother and sister-in-law," he said, and Pete shook their hands. "And my sister, Sabrina."

"Nice to meet you," Pete said politely as he shook Sabrina's hand.

"Aren't the renovations divine?" Amelia said, taking in the tall windows that reached almost to the ceiling, which was two stories high.

"We're pleased with them," Avery said, her eyes brimming with happiness as she, too, admired the handiwork.

Amelia faced Avery. "You played a part in this?"

"I did a bit of work with the architects and designers who did the renovations."

Amelia inclined her head. "How generous of you."

"Not really," Sabrina said. "We enjoy the arts. We have several galleries in our neighborhood but this one holds a special place in our hearts. So, we're fairly healthy contributors."

"It does host some of the best events," Amelia agreed. But her eyes drifted to Harper and then Seth. They narrowed a fraction of an inch, then they lowered to gaze at their hands.

Even as Seth noticed that, he also saw that Jake had his free hand on the small of Avery's back. Possessive. But also, affectionate.

Seth smoothly raised his hand to the bottom of Harper's back. Harper shifted closer to him, as if she too had seen her mother's curious gaze.

"Who has the baby?"

"Seth's neighbor, Mrs. Petrillo."

Amelia's eyebrows rose. "*Seth's* neighbor?"

He let Amelia figure that one out for herself. If he and Harper really were dating, they'd be spending the night together. And if they were spending the night together, who better to keep Crystal than the woman next door?

Seth knew the minute Amelia pieced it all together. Her slim lips tipped up into a pleased smile.

Harper's mother liked him. If he and Harper were dating for real, Harper wouldn't ever again have to worry about her mom's feelings for Clark.

The man behind Jake tapped him on the shoulder and when Jake turned he said, "Jimmy! My gosh! How long has it been?"

Avery turned, too.

Sabrina mumbled something about needing to find her boyfriend, one of the artists whose work was being exhibited.

As Harper and Seth spoke with her parents, Jake and Avery drifted into the crowd. Then Amelia and Pete excused themselves to mingle. Seth followed Harper as she walked among the exhibits, thoroughly engrossed in the art and thoroughly enjoying herself.

The way she should. The way he *wanted* her to.

At eleven, Harper reminded Seth that they'd promised Mrs. P. they'd be back by eleven-thirty, so she could get into her pajamas to watch a movie that was playing that night.

They walked toward the door, Harper's mom's eyes following them, and nearly plowed into his mother.

"Seth, Harper." She smiled warmly as she took in their clasped hands. "I hope you enjoyed the evening."

"Most fun I've had in a long time, Mrs. Mc-Callan."

"There's another event coming up in a few weeks, a ball. I think you'll enjoy that, too."

Harper reluctantly said, "We'll see," but Seth thought that was a fine idea. The more they got out, into dating situations, the more they'd be able to decide if they shouldn't make this real.

"We'll definitely be at the ball."

His mom smiled. "Good!"

They stepped out into the night air and Seth motioned to the valet.

"Are you sure going to a ball is a good idea?"

"We're dating. There's a ball." He almost laughed at his own cleverness. "You do the math. If we don't go, people will wonder."

The valet roared up in his Ferrari. The top was down but he didn't make a move to put it up.

When they were settled, he pressed the gas pedal to send the powerful car careening down the street. The moon was full, the air still warm as summer held on. Her laughter wove through him, pleasing him, relaxing him.

And he couldn't remember why he'd been fighting this.

Harper couldn't contain the joy that bubbled up and spilled out, as the glorious car roared up the nearly empty streets. She loved the Ferrari, the smooth speed that took them effortlessly from stoplight to stoplight. But most of all she marveled at the ease of luxury. How simple life was when one had a good family and friends.

She wished the drive could go on forever, but she had a baby to care for, so when Seth pulled his beautiful car into the basement parking garage, she didn't sigh with disappointment.

She also didn't correct Seth when he put his hand on the small of her back, guiding her into the elevator. It wasn't easy to pretend they were together one minute and jump apart the next. She could understand his slipup. But she also had to admit it had felt pretty good to have his undivided attention that night. True, most of his actions were directed toward making sure her mother believed they were dating. But sometimes it felt as if they really were dating.

After a glass of champagne, she had to keep reminding herself they weren't.

He hit the button for the elevator to take them to his condo. She combed her fingers through her windblown hair.

He caught her hand. "Don't."

"Don't?"

"I like it sort of crazy like that."

She did, too.

Their gazes met.

He smiled.

Her insides trembled.

He stood near enough that she could touch him, and her fingers itched to. All she'd have to do is raise her hand to his face and run her fingers along the rough shadow of dark hair that had begun on his cheeks. She knew he was off-limits, Clark's friend whose money allowed him to date any woman he wanted. But she hadn't had this intense longing to touch someone in over a year. Fresh and surprising, it rippled along her nerve endings and tumbled to her fingertips.

"What's going on in that head of yours?"

She shook her head at the silliness of her thoughts. "Nothing."

"Didn't look like nothing."

That's when she realized he still held her hand. They weren't even two feet apart. And she wanted to touch him.

The elevator seemed to slow to a crawl.

He inched closer. "It looked a lot like something. And it made you smile." His lips curved upward. "Really smile. I know you enjoyed the ride in the Ferrari. I think you enjoyed the night. You wouldn't by any chance be considering giving me a good-night kiss to thank me?"

Her heart stumbled as her gaze fell to his full mouth. Funny how she'd never noticed how sensuous his mouth was. She should have. The memory of those lips on hers the day they'd run into her mom should have told her his mouth wasn't just plentiful; it was clever.

But so was she. Even if he was attracted to her, she'd already worked all this out in her head. Starting something with him wasn't right. No matter how lonely she'd been. She still missed Clark. That wasn't any way to start a relationship. Plus, he wasn't the kind of guy she'd date. Even as she told herself she needed to get them out of this, her heart pinched. Something about walking away from him just didn't seem right.

Still, when the elevator reached their floor, she slid her hand from his and stepped out into the hall, striding toward his condo door.

"You know as soon as Mrs. P. leaves you and I will be alone."

Oh, she knew that. And her pattering heart almost exploded with the possibilities. None of which she was ready for. None of which seemed any more right than walking away had seemed.

He walked up behind her and slid his arm across her body to put his key into the lock. His scent drifted to her and she could almost feel the heat of his body on her back.

Hard as it was, she wouldn't let herself shudder. Refused to let her mind go blank and her senses kick in. This man would kiss her tonight and call a girlfriend in the morning—

All the same...she couldn't remember ever feeling like this with a man. Part of her really wanted to see it through. Tease him. Kiss him again...

Mrs. P. opened the door. "Get in here, you goofs. My next movie is about to start." She edged past them into the hall as they walked inside the condo. "Baby was good. An angel. But she hasn't even stirred so my guess it you'll be getting a two- or three-a.m. wake-up call."

And that was reality. Harper wasn't the woman who dated playboys, indulged in their games, amused herself.

She was a mom.

A widow and a mom.

She also wasn't a coward.

Fortifying herself with a deep breath, she faced

Seth. "I did have a good time." When she heard Mrs. Petrillo's condo door close, she added, "I did want a good-night kiss." And everything it might have led to. "Not because I'm crazy for you or even to thank you, but because I'm curious. I don't think you'd take advantage of that because I'd be a willing participant. But that doesn't make it right. You were Clark's best friend."

CHAPTER SIX

SHE TURNED AND walked to her bedroom, leaving Seth standing in the little space between his kitchen island and the living room. Challenge rolled through him, but it was tempered by something that stopped him cold. She was right. He wouldn't take advantage of her, but not because she would be a willing participant. Because he liked her. That's why he'd flirted with her. Teased her. Why he'd had the urge to toss caution to the wind.

He shook his head once, as annoyance with himself became red-hot anger.

Was he falling for her again?

No matter that he'd stepped back all those years ago and let Clark ask her out, he'd loved her. But even as a twenty-two-year-old, he'd known he was damaged goods. He hadn't become a playboy because he loved women—though he did. He'd become a playboy because he knew he couldn't settle down and he didn't want anyone to get hurt. Not even him.

Now, here he was, tempting himself with emotions he wasn't allowed to feel. With a woman he wasn't allowed to have. Which was crazy.

Still, lust had roared through him when she'd said she was curious. Since they'd already kissed that had to mean she was curious about other things. That had taken his brain straight to the gutter. Because he was curious about those other things, too. How different would it be to make love to a woman who wasn't just a friend, but was somebody he loved?

Had loved. Past tense. He might be getting new feelings for her, or resurrecting the old feelings, but now that he was aware he could stop them in their tracks. He did not want to hurt her. And he didn't want to find himself in a situation he couldn't get out of. A prison. To him that's what marriage was. He could see himself marrying Harper, simply so he wouldn't hurt her, and then living a life in a cage…or becoming his dad. A cheat. A man who justified being unfaithful because he was bored.

A cold chill sliced through him.

He would not be his dad.

Never.
Not ever.

He left the condo early Sunday morning, but the scent of her perfume from the night before lingered in the air and followed him to his car. Annoyed, he punched the accelerator and headed for the family beach house in Montauk for some time alone.

The huge, empty McCallan mansion gave him some perspective as his solitary footsteps echoed around him. He was a man meant to be alone. He loved solitude. He liked his own company. He didn't need to be around people. But when he wanted to, he could. He had tons of friends, and women loved him.

One of the family limos pulled up and his mom exited. Morris, the older driver his mother favored, followed her up the walk carrying bags as if she'd been shopping.

When they opened the door and saw him standing in the echoing foyer, they both jumped.

His mother said, "What are you doing here?"

He rolled his shoulders. "Looking for some peace and quiet. What are you doing here?"

She motioned for Morris to take the enormous bags to the kitchen down the hall. "I found the most adorable new cushions for the lounge around the fire-pit table on the back deck."

"And you had to bring them here today?"

Not happy with the challenge, his other's eyes narrowed. "Where's Harper?"

"With Crystal." *Clark's daughter.* Clark's baby girl. The child his friend had always wanted.

His resolve to not get involved with Harper strengthened. He might have to play his role, but he also didn't want his mom to get her hopes up. His time with Harper would definitely end. He didn't want questions or, worse, a scolding.

"Our relationship is casual." He shrugged. "I don't think it's going to lead to anything. Two weeks from now, we might not even be dating."

"You don't like her?" his mom asked, breezily heading toward the kitchen. "Or Crystal?"

The suggestion that he didn't like Crystal infuriated him. For a little squirmy thing she was no trouble. "If you're saying that I'd never settle down with Harper because she's a mom, you're wrong. There's nothing wrong with Harper or the baby. I'm just never getting married. And you of all people should know that."

"Seriously? You're still saying that?"

Fury rolled through him again. He knew it was time to back down, walk away before he said something they'd both regret. But he wouldn't let her brush his miserable childhood aside. "Yes. I'm still saying that. Because it's true." He rolled his shoulders again, trying to get rid of a tightness that wouldn't let go today. "You know what? You enjoy the day. I'm going back to the city."

She sighed. "Don't leave on my account. We could do something together. Maybe play Scrabble or take a walk on the beach."

The things they'd done when his dad was MIA? "No thanks. I've gotta run."

He was at the front door before he realized he had nowhere to go and nothing to do. On a normal weekend, he'd have had dates lined up or fishing trips with friends. He might even be in Monte Carlo, just for the hell of it. To keep up this ruse for Harper, he'd bowed out of everything.

Antsy, he ambled to his car. Not only had he been edged out of his home, but the big house he'd hoped to be his sanctuary was also off-limits.

He managed to stay out all day by taking a

long drive, getting dinner at a bistro close to his home and taking a walk to stretch his legs, only returning to the condo after he was sure Harper was already in her room for the night.

But seeing her sunny smile on Monday morning, he stopped dead in his tracks. Warming a bottle in his kitchen, she looked beautiful and sexy, slim and sensual in those soft blue pajamas that were probably still warm from sleep.

His feelings from Saturday night returned. That he liked her. That he wanted to make this real—along with her declaration that she wanted nothing to do with him.

Because of Clark. His friend.

"Okay. I have some early meetings," he said, forgoing coffee for a quick escape. "I'll see you after I get home tonight."

He raced to the front door, hearing her say, "Okay. 'Bye."

But the image of leaving her confused, standing by the kitchen island, burned in his brain. By the time he got to the office, he knew something had to be done about their situation. If proximity was causing him to get real feelings for her, then proximity was what he had to fix. He couldn't kick her out. But she would move once she had a job.

He'd already called the one friend who might have had an opening for an assistant. That had failed.

He decided on another route and marched to the Human Resources office.

Karen, Mary Martin's assistant, looked up. "Mr. McCallan!"

"I'd like to see Mary for a few minutes, if I can."

"Sure!" She tapped a few buttons on her phone, told Mary he was there and within seconds Mary's door opened. Fiftysomething with kind green eyes, she motioned him inside her office.

"What brings you here?"

He took the seat in front of her desk as she sat on her tall-backed chair behind it. "I have a friend who needs a job."

"We put a moratorium on hiring until February."

"I know. But I'm trying to help my friend and I don't know enough about the kind of job she wants to really understand how to assist her."

"What kind of work does she want?"

"Administrative or personal assistant."

"Lots of jobs like that out there."

He stifled a sigh of relief. Hope built. Maybe with Mary's help he could get Harper a job and put her out of range of temptation. "Good."

"What are her qualifications?"

"She ran a personal-assistant-type company before she married my friend. She walked dogs, planned parties, sent birthday gifts for guys too busy to buy them, that kind of thing."

Mary sat back. "Oh."

His hope crumbled itself into a ball and tossed itself into the trash can. "That was a bad 'oh.'"

"She doesn't have any *office* experience. She's probably going to have to start at the bottom somewhere."

"As what?"

"Clerk, typist, mail room."

His hope peered out of the trash can. "She's willing to do anything."

"She also needs to be willing to start at the bottom of the pay scale."

Knowing Harper wasn't picky, Seth and his hope perked up. "How low is bottom?"

She named a figure and he sucked in a breath. His hope collapsed and died. "She'll never support herself on that."

"No one can. Most people starting out get a roommate."

That's what he'd done. Two years *after* graduating university, he and Ziggy still needed to live together. He couldn't get his own place until the investment firm he and Clark started had become successful. Now that Mary had him thinking back to his very humble beginnings, he realized it didn't matter what Harper did. The only work she could do would not support her and a baby.

She was going to have to tell her mom…live with her mom.

The possibility upset him almost as much as he knew it would upset Harper.

He left Mary's office and ambled to his own, trying to think this through. The easy answer would be for her to let him buy her a condo, but if she wouldn't let him buy her a few sweaters, she'd never let him buy her a place to live.

He could afford a hundred houses and she wouldn't let him buy her one measly house—

He *could* afford a hundred houses. He could buy a condo, a beach house, a house in Connecticut… He could buy *anything* he wanted.

Maybe *that* was the answer.

He'd tell her *he* wanted a new place, something bigger or maybe an actual house, and his condo would be open. She'd never take it as a gift, but he could have an agreement drawn up where he sold her the condo interest-free and she paid him a minimal amount every month.

He'd make the deal sufficient that she would know he wasn't *giving* her his condo, but also so sweet she wouldn't be able to resist it.

He laughed. Once he found himself a place, their separation wouldn't depend on her finding a job. Though he would still help her find work. He just wouldn't be doing it while sleeping in the next room. He'd be in another condo or a house a state away.

He went home happy. Not because he wanted to be away from her, but because he didn't want to hurt her. He didn't like the idea that hormones or mixed-up feelings from the past or even proximity would lure him into something he couldn't get out of without hurting her. Or getting hurt himself. Finding himself a new place was the perfect answer.

He walked into his condo whistling. "Hey, I had a thought today."

Occupied with tucking the baby into her carrier, Harper peeked over. "You did?"

"You know how you need a house?"

"Yes."

"I also need a house."

At that she stopped tucking the blanket around Crystal and peered at him. "What?"

"Look around you. This is the condo of a guy who's got a little money but he's also frugal."

She gaped at him. "It's a beautiful place."

"I'm not saying it's not beautiful. I'm saying it doesn't suit me anymore."

"Oh. You want something a little more *McCallan*."

He winced. "No. I'd been tossing around the idea of getting a new home. I bought this about a year after Clark and I started the investment firm. I still didn't know if we'd make it or not. Then two years ago my dad died, and I'm not going to lie, Harper, I inherited some money."

"Seth, there's no crime in that. For people who have a ton of money, you and your family are very nice. Very normal."

Very normal? He almost laughed. He'd spent his childhood listening to his parents argue, his teen years being bullied by his dad and his adulthood avoiding all of it until Jake—the brother he loved and trusted—asked him for help running the family business and he'd agreed.

"Anyway, I realized I could sell this one to you."

She gasped. "Oh, Seth. I can't afford this."

"I know. Theoretically, you can't afford *anything* until you get a job." Or even after she got a job, but she'd realize that soon enough. "But here's the deal. I can sell you this and finance it for you."

"What?"

"I'll have my lawyer draw up papers that transfer ownership to you in return for you paying me a certain amount every month until the value of the condo is reached."

"You mean never."

He shook his head. "Most mortgages take forever to pay off because of interest. I was thinking of not charging you interest."

"You can't do that!"

"Why not?"

"It's too generous!"

"Hey, what Clark did for me saved me." Another thing he needed to remember when touching Harper tempted him. "Besides, there are other strings attached to this deal."

"What strings?"

"I have money but very little time. You have time on your hands. It would help me if you'd meet with a real estate agent and weed out the bad properties, so I'd only have to see the ones that really were contenders."

Her face brightened. "I'd do that for nothing… as your friend."

"You made my case for no interest. Just as you would help me find a house or a bigger condo because you're my friend. I should be allowed to sell you this place and finance it with no interest because I'm your friend."

"You're not going to bamboozle me."

"No. But you're not going to change my mind about no interest." He sighed. "This works for both of us, Harper. Take the deal."

The following morning, Mrs. Petrillo was happy to watch the baby while Harper and Seth met with Bill Reynolds, a real estate agent recommended to Seth by a friend. Rather than meet in his office, Bill suggested they get together at an empty condo not far from Seth's current home in Midtown. Harper might be the one doing the actual legwork of finding Seth a new place to live, but Bill wanted Seth to see a few condos, so he could get an idea of what Seth wanted.

When Seth and Harper arrived at the building, it was easy to see it had been renovated, but it had been done in such a way as to keep the "old Manhattan" charm of things like fleur-de-lis crown molding, pocket doors, elegant chandeliers and reclaimed hardwood floors.

Harper's face lit up when they rode the old-fashioned elevator to the top floor. But when she saw Bill Reynolds, her eyes widened. Dressed in a dark suit and white shirt with a slim tie, he wasn't buttoned down. His jacket swung open when he reached out to shake Seth's hand and his tie had been loosened.

Seth supposed the real estate agent's intent had been to look approachable but for some reason or another it got on Seth's nerves.

"It's a pleasure to meet you, Mr. McCallan."

"It's Seth."

"Seth," Bill said amiably. He turned to Harper. "And this is Harper?"

"Yes. She's the friend who will be helping me find a new home."

Seth swore the man didn't hear a word after Seth said, "She's the friend."

His eyebrows rose, and his smile grew as he shook Harper's hand. "I don't suppose you're looking for a place?"

"She's taking my current condo," Seth said, moving from the entryway into the living room. A white fireplace drew his eye first. Dark sofas sat parallel to each other atop a yellow area rug. End tables were thick, old wood. Lamps were dusty. Drapes hid the view.

"Look beyond the furniture, Seth," Harper said, walking to the window. "That crown molding is beautiful." She pulled open the drapes and gasped. "The view is fantastic. Everything else is cosmetic."

Bill inclined his head. "You're very smart about this stuff."

"No. I spent a year house hunting with my husband."

Bill deflated. "Your husband?"

"Deceased," Harper said quietly.

"I am so sorry," Bill said, but Seth didn't believe he meant a word of it. He gave Bill the side eye. Dark hair. Sharp green eyes, so colorful they had to be contacts. Clean shaven. Good suit.

Though New York claimed to be a city for all people, there were tiers of society. Seth and his family sat on the top tier with only a few other extraordinarily wealthy families. Below them was a tier of people almost as wealthy as the McCallans. Below that was a tier of people still wealthy enough not to have to work, but with less money than the two tiers above them. Below them were what Seth called the working rich.

That's where Bill fit. If Seth bought a condo through Bill, his commission would be high six figures, maybe even seven. Sell eight or ten condos a year with that kind of commission and you earned yourself a place at good restaurants, charity fund-raisers, private parties attended by only the elite.

But though Bill wasn't truly wealthy, he was Harper's type. A man who worked hard to make something of himself.

Seth wanted to hate him but couldn't. *That's* what Seth had been, when he'd left home. That's what Harper had liked—maybe even what she'd loved about Clark. Harper had hated the life of luxury without substance. Clark had had substance. Hard-working real estate agent Bill had substance.

They breezed through a formal dining room, a den, an open kitchen desperately in need of a remodel and a maid's suite, then to a hidden set of stairs that led to three guestrooms and a generous master suite.

"I don't need all these rooms."

Bill laughed. "Of course, you don't. But space is money in the city. If you're paying twenty-five million dollars, you should get something to show for it." He pointed at French doors that led to a balcony. "Like that. Imagine that view at night."

He saw the skyline and knew that when it was dark, with hundreds of lights twinkling in the surrounding buildings, it was probably amazing. "I'm not the kind of guy who's going to stand out on the balcony in my pajamas—"

"None of which matters," Harper interrupted. "Because this place needs too much remodeling for you."

Seth faced her. "It does?"

"Yes." She smiled at him and he felt a little better. Not quite the snob Bill made him feel like. "If your condo furnishings are anything to go by, you like clean lines. You also like an open floorplan."

Bill brightened. "I have just the thing for you. Two buildings down. Open concept. Kind of modified industrial."

They left the condo and walked up the street to the building. Seth wasn't happy with that home, either. He also didn't like the third place Bill showed them.

Driving home, Harper said, "I think what you really didn't like was Bill."

Seth glanced out the window. "He was pretentious."

"He was trying to make a living."

"Actually, I think he was buttering me up, hoping to make an easy sale. He said we were only going out in order that he could get an idea of what I wanted but he thought I'd buy one of those three."

"Well, you didn't, and now that he's seen your taste, he'll try harder next time." She smiled again, and Seth felt better again.

"Besides, you won't have to go condo hunting until I narrow the choices down to two or three places I genuinely believe you will love."

He said, "That's good," then remembered she'd be alone with Bill Reynolds. Ambitious, centered, normal guy, Bill Reynolds.

Jealousy slithered through him like green slime. Sticky. Hot. Uncomfortable. He tried to shrug it off, but slime didn't shrug off easily.

"Maybe I should come with you?"

"You don't trust me?"

Damn. "Of course, I trust you."

She caught his gaze. "Then trust me to work with Bill."

He wondered if there was a double meaning behind what she said, then called himself an idiot. He couldn't have her. She'd been Clark's. He also wouldn't put himself into a position where he could become like his dad. So, what did it matter if she found another man interesting?

He stopped the Ferrari in front of the condo building and waited while she exited. She waved goodbye and walked inside, and he didn't stare after her like somebody so weak he didn't know good from bad. In a roundabout way, his dad had taught him good from bad. He'd married Seth's mom, but he hadn't been faithful. Seth had seen his mom cry, heard their fights. All because his dad had a roving eye and not one clue about loyalty or honesty. Especially not honesty with himself.

Seth shot off in the direction of McCallan, Inc. He was honest enough with himself not to pine after a woman he couldn't have, even if loneliness unexpectedly filled his soul.

CHAPTER SEVEN

THAT AFTERNOON, Harper called Bill Reynolds to discuss more homes for viewing. He pointed out six listings on the real estate company's website, she chose three and they arranged to see all three the next day.

She made Seth a special dinner. They'd almost made a huge mistake after the cocktail party. She'd wanted to touch him so much, she'd ached from it. But their being together was a bad idea.

Whatever he'd done on Sunday had helped him to accept that. He'd even happily decided *he* was the one who needed a new home. So, when he'd seemed horribly out of sorts while Bill showed them the condos, she worried it was because he was having second thoughts about moving. She appreciated his helping her get a place for herself and Crystal, and as long as he really did let her pay him for his condo, she wanted it. But if he had even one inkling of doubt about doing this, she wouldn't let him sell his home to her.

With the baby sitting in her carrier and dinner served, she casually said, "So, I made arrangements to see three more condos tomorrow."

He sucked in a breath. "Did you?"

Sucked in breath? Eyes down? That added up to avoidance. She was correct. He wasn't happy.

"Two are gorgeous. If they meet my standards, they might be contenders. The other one is actually two condos that could be combined into one."

He peeked at her. "That would mean renovations."

"I added it because I saw terrific potential. If you wouldn't mind a bit of renovating, you could really make that place yours."

"No. No renovations. I want move-in ready."

"Okay, I won't look at that one then."

His face registered relief. "So, you'd only be looking at two?"

That was confusing. Why would he possibly be happy there were only two condos instead of three? If he really didn't want a different home, he wouldn't want her looking at anything.

She had no choice but to push him to either stop knocking houses off the list or to admit he didn't want her looking at anything.

"Maybe I'll only look at one, if the first one is good."

His face brightened again. "If you like this first one a lot, maybe I should just come with you? That way if we both like it I can take it."

That didn't fit with either idea.

She set her fork down. "Seth, you don't want to buy the first thing you see. Options are good."

"Options mean more time."

"That's why I'm going out with Bill for the first look at every property. To weed out the ones that for sure wouldn't work."

"Yeah. I get it." He bounded out of his seat. "You know what? I'm kind of tired tonight. And there's a game on. I'm just going to go watch that."

He started down the hall, but she caught up with him. "Wait a minute. You have to tell me what's wrong."

"There is nothing wrong except I had a long day and I'm tired and there's a game on."

She studied his eyes. They didn't even flicker. But there was a shadow of something in them. Actually, it could be exhaustion.

Maybe he was right? Maybe he was fine. Tired, but fine.

Still, standing this close all her feelings from the night of the cocktail party crept up on her. Something about him drew her. Made her pulse jump and all her longings rise, reminding her that being with a man she loved was wonderful.

But they'd already talked about this. She'd told him anything between them was wrong and he'd listened.

Maybe that was what was going on now? He'd flirted with her on Saturday night and she'd rebuffed him. She'd told a sweet, sexy guy she didn't want him. She didn't think she'd hurt him, but she had said she didn't want anything to start between them.

Maybe he was keeping his distance because she'd asked him to?

Disappointment filled her. But she was the one who had nixed a relationship.

Because they weren't a good match.

She took a step back, away from him. They weren't right for each other. But they were still friends. He was kind enough to sell her his condo and she liked the idea of doing some work to help him find a new place to live. If she wanted their friendship to survive, maybe she had to stop pushing.

"Okay. Good night."

"Good night."

Wednesday morning, he was gone before she and Crystal came out of her bedroom. Knowing it was better for them to each have some personal space, she fed Crystal, ate breakfast, dressed to meet Bill at the first house and said goodbye to Mrs. Petrillo, who had agreed to stay with the baby.

She met Bill at the condo building, rode up in the elevator with him and strode down the hall like a businesswoman doing a job.

Just the thought straightened her spine with confidence. She'd liked working. Not for money, but to have a place in society. To provide a service. The task Seth probably considered a throwaway job reminded her of the sense of purpose that she'd missed for the five years she and Clark had been married.

Bill unlocked the door and presented the space to her.

"Oh." She carefully eased into the beautiful home. "It's lovely."

Bill followed her. "I didn't think old-style charm suited Mr. McCallan. But this modern floorplan does."

She took in the gray hardwood floors, white wood trim, paler gray walls and modern furniture. "It's gorgeous."

They walked down a hall to the bedrooms. The entire condo was perfect. Very suited to Seth with clean lines and neutral tones that allowed for more colorful furniture and window treatments.

Riding down in the elevator, she told Bill that she definitely thought this one was a contender and he grinned.

"Good." He paused for a second then said, "So how do you know the McCallans?"

"My husband was Seth's best friend."

His smile warmed. "I see."

"I'm helping him find a new home and he's helping me with a few things."

Bill sniffed a laugh. "Don't be angry but I thought the two of you might be dating."

She pictured it. Having private dinners on the balcony of a gorgeous penthouse overlooking the city. Teaching him to love Crystal. More kisses like the first one they'd shared.

Her heart stuttered. Not just because the images gave her a warm, happy feeling, but because for a second, she'd forgotten about Clark.

She took a calming breath to steady her heart and ease the guilt. "No. Just friends."

"Well, that's good news for me then."

She frowned. "It is?"

"It means I can ask you out."

Ask her out?

He was attracted to her?

"Oh." The oddest sensation wound through her. Anytime Seth was close, her shivers were the good kind. This feeling wasn't like that. It wasn't revulsion. It was more like confusion mixed with lack of interest.

And once again, Clark wasn't anywhere in the picture.

This time when her heart squeezed, it wasn't from the thrill of being around Seth. It was her soul's gentle reminder that Clark kept falling out of the picture because he was gone. Had been for a year. The shock and sadness that had enveloped her immediately after his death had lessened to a dull ache that felt more like a memory than real pain.

She swallowed back the sorrow of that. It felt like the last step in losing him.

"That's very nice of you, but I'm not dating right now. My husband's only been dead a year.

I'm just getting back in the world of work. I'm not ready yet."

He flipped a card from his jacket pocket and handed it to her in one smooth movement. "When you are, give me a call."

She smiled and took the card but the realization that Clark was gone—really gone—pressed down on her chest. It wasn't pain. She would have welcomed pain. But an empty, awful awareness that this stage was the end. And she really was alone.

Except for Seth. Kind. Generous. Seth.

Whom she'd given the brushoff after the cocktail party.

Her chest tightened, but she ignored it. She might be adjusting to Clark's death, easing him and their life together into a memory, but that didn't mean she was ready to date. Especially not someone like Seth. Social. Outgoing. Playboy.

She frowned. Those things were supposed to set her straight about him. Instead, she remembered being in his car, the wind in her hair—

No. Seth wasn't right for her.

Bill showed her two other homes, one of which was a maybe, but the third one that he'd added on the fly was a definite no.

By the time she was back at Seth's condo, soon to be *her* condo, it was nearly seven.

Seth and Mrs. Petrillo sat on the sofa, watching *Wheel of Fortune*, with baby Crystal tucked in her carrier, sitting between them.

"Hey."

All eyes turned to her.

"Sorry, it took longer than I expected. But the good news is, I think two of the condos he showed me today would be perfect for you."

She walked over to the sofa and lifted Crystal out of the carrier. Her little girl grinned at her. "I know why you're grinning. You should be getting ready for bed."

Mrs. Petrillo slapped her knees and hoisted herself from the sofa. "And this is my cue to leave." As she passed Harper, she whispered, "Seth told me it was okay to let her stay up."

Harper laughed. "She's fine. As long as I get her to bed by eight, I'm happy."

Mrs. Petrillo shuffled out the door and Harper turned to Seth. "I noticed that you didn't comment when I said I thought we might have found two condos suited to you."

"That's great."

"You don't sound like you think it's great."

"That's because I'm not sure I don't want a house rather than a condo. Someplace like Connecticut or Montauk."

The change surprised her enough that she forgot about herself, losing Clark and even being attracted to Seth. Though money wasn't changing hands, he'd hired her to help him. And she wanted to do this. Not just to get an interest-free home, but to pay him back for all the kindnesses he'd extended to her.

"Okay. I'll talk to Bill about it."

Seth rose from the sofa. "No. I'll talk to him. I'll call him tomorrow."

Confusion skittered through her. First, he was changing what he wanted, now he was edging her out? "Isn't that what I'm supposed to be doing for you?"

"No. You're taking the first look at what he comes up with." His voice was cool, serious.

All the fears she'd had the night before trembled back, sprinkled with the sense that he was trying to get away from her—or wanted nothing to do with her.

"What I'd like in a house is different than what I'd need in something in the city. Once I tell Bill, he'll find a few things. Then you're on the job again."

She nodded, but something odd filled the air.

"After you take care of Crystal then we can figure out what to do for dinner. I was thinking maybe a pizza."

"Pizza sounds great." She took Crystal back to her bedroom. As she changed the baby into pajamas, she tried to figure out what the odd thing was. She replayed all the conversations she and Seth had had since she'd moved in with him. He'd kissed her once—as part of a charade. The one time he had flirted with her, after the cocktail party, she'd told him she wanted nothing to do with him.

And now he wasn't mad. But he wasn't happy, either. And why would he be? He was stuck in the same house with a woman who'd rebuffed him.

She had to find him somewhere to live—and quickly—before they grew to dislike each other.

In his office Thursday morning, Seth heard the sound of Jake and Sabrina laughing. His brow wrinkled. Sabrina never came to McCallan, Inc. She wanted no part of the family business and, given their history, Jake and Seth had understood.

Curiosity overwhelmed him, and he rose from his tall-back leather chair and strode out into the private reception area for the executive offices.

"Seth!" Sabrina raced over and kissed his cheek. "In all the mess after the showing over the weekend, I forgot to give you a new invitation to my exhibit on Saturday."

He pulled the embossed card from the white envelope. A McCallan didn't need an invitation to get into anything, except... He saw the name of the gallery—in Paris—and winced. "I'd forgotten all about this."

Sabrina's face fell. "You have to come! Pierre is flipping out. It's the first time we've done an exhibit alone together. It's the first time he's done an exhibit alone with *anyone*. Honestly, Seth, I worry he might just bail at the last minute and then it'll be Sally. All by herself."

Seth glanced up from his invitation. "Would that be so bad?"

Her face filled with horror. "He's the star. I'm the also-ran. If he bails, the exhibit is canceled. I'll need a shoulder to cry on."

"You'll have Jake."

Jake shook his head. "We're leaving early. Avery has a trial."

Sabina turned pleading blue eyes on him. "If Avery and Jake can squeeze me in around a trial, whatever you have can be canceled."

"I…" He sucked in a breath, palming the invitation, which included Harper. He didn't know how this would go over with Harper, but the addition of her name to the invitation was more than a clue that Sabrina expected her there, too. And maybe being across an ocean, with Jake and Avery and Sabrina, would be better than running around the city all weekend, trying to figure out reasons to stay out of his apartment. "Sure."

Sabrina impulsively hugged him. "Thanks."

"You're welcome."

"And bring Harper's little girl."

Jake said, "That's a great idea. We've hired a nanny for Friday night and Saturday. She can keep Crystal, too. That'll give Abby someone to play with."

"Crystal's not much on playing. She basically sits in a carrier when she isn't sleeping."

"That's even better. That'll give Abby a chance to adjust to being around a baby for when Avery and I decide it's time to have another."

As Sabrina turned to the elevator, Jake headed back to his office and Seth stood alone in the quiet reception area.

Not only were he and Harper going to France, but it also appeared they were taking the baby.

How was he going to tell Harper they'd be spending the weekend in Paris? Leaving that night so they'd have Friday to adjust to the time change and be ready for the Saturday afternoon showing.

He called her. "I have something that might not be good news."

A light sigh drifted from his phone. "You decided you didn't want to move."

He shook his head, realizing that she thought of a lot of life in negative terms. Maybe because hers had been so difficult. First, a demanding mom, then losing her husband, then finding out their financial situation had been a lie.

"No. We're going to Paris this weekend."

"What?"

"My sister has a showing. Unless we want our secret to get out, we have to go. The whole family had promised we'd be there for her when Sabrina made these arrangements." He shook his head. "It kind of snuck up on me. Sorry."

She laughed. "You're sorry that you're taking me to Paris?" She gasped. "Oh. I can't go. I have Crystal!"

"Jake would like her to come along. He's got a nanny for Abby and he'd also like Abby to be around a baby. I think he and Avery are thinking of having another one."

"Crystal gets to come along?"

"I hope she's got a party dress."

Harper laughed. "I'm sorry, Seth, to be so excited about something that's probably a burden for you, but I've never been to France!"

"You haven't?"

"No. My parents didn't start traveling until after I left home."

"Okay, then. Pack appropriately."

"Do you think Avery would mind if I called to see what I need to bring?"

"I don't see why. She likes you." He winced. "Oh, and one more little thing. We're leaving tonight."

"Tonight! Good grief, Seth! I'll talk to you later! I have to call Avery and pack."

They flew to Paris with Avery, Jake and little Abby, and slept through most of the flight—without a problem or complicated explanation because Seth and Harper volunteered to take the bedroom with twin beds and give the jet's master suite to Avery and Jake. Though they'd left New York at eleven o'clock at night, given the flight time and the time difference, they arrived in Paris in the early afternoon.

They piled into the limo, which had two car seats already installed, and Harper secretly marveled at the ease of it.

The brothers joked about staying at the Four Seasons because their mother stayed at the Bristol and Avery sighed. "Your mother is lovely."

Jake said, "I know that. It's just that no man wants to stay in the same hotel as his mom when he's away from work." He gave Avery a significant look. "We want to have some fun."

Avery laughed.

Harper struggled not to gape at them. No matter how much time she spent with Avery and Jake, she still couldn't believe how normal they were. Or how equal they were. Jake managed behemoth McCallan, Inc., yet Avery's career as a small-town lawyer was every bit as important. They shared baby chores. Jake grilled burgers, hot dogs or steak once a week. And though they had a penthouse on the Upper East Side, they spent most of their time at a house in Pennsylvania.

The group checked in at the Four Seasons and separated when Seth and Harper got off on the floor of their suite and Jake and Avery rode to the penthouse.

Harper tried not to gape at the luxurious suite, but it was no use. The place was amazing. The door had opened onto a living room with pale furniture, bowls of white roses scattered everywhere and views of the city that took her breath away.

"There are two bedrooms. My assistant also ordered a crib."

At the mention of his assistant, Harper held back a wince. She might be staying the weekend in a suite like this, but next month she'd be the one ordering the crib for some other lucky family.

"We should get breakfast. It might be afternoon in Paris, but we're still on New York time."

Carrying sleeping Crystal, Harper opened the first bedroom door and saw a crib in the fabulous bedroom with a thick blue comforter and white furniture. With the pale blue curtains open, she had another view of the city.

She almost couldn't wrap her mind around the fact that she was in Paris. That Seth's family apparently flew here all the time. That their life didn't revolve around making money.

She faced Seth and said, "Sure. Breakfast is a great idea."

Seth eyed her shrewdly. "What's up?"

"I'm just a little blown away by it all."

He slipped out of his black leather jacket. "It is nice."

"It's amazing." His whole life was amazing. He worked, but it wasn't his life. He could have anything he wanted but he was down-to-earth. Maybe more than Clark had been.

He laughed. "Does that mean you want to go *out* to eat?"

"Avery said your mom has plans for dinner this evening. Crystal will be staying with the nanny for that. So maybe it would be best if we ate here." She paused then said, "If there's somewhere you want to go, you can. I just don't like to leave her for long stretches of time and she'll be getting up from her nap soon."

He plopped to the expensive sofa as if it were a beanbag chair. "Then I'll stay, too."

"You don't have to."

"Hey, we're supposed to be a couple. I can't go prowling Paris like a single guy."

She nodded. But her heart took a tumble. Just as she'd be somebody's assistant in another month, she'd also be away from Seth.

"For the weekend, let's be a couple. Let's do what we'd do if we really were dating so that there won't be any slipups with my mom."

"All right."

He angled his feet on the gorgeous cut-glass coffee table. "What would you and Crystal do on an afternoon in Paris?"

She thought about that for a second. "After I ate, I'd probably see if I could get a stroller and take Crystal around the city."

"See how simple that was?"

She laughed. "I suppose."

They ordered breakfast and just as they were finishing eating, Crystal woke. Harper brought her out and fed her a bottle, as Seth called the concierge for a stroller.

It arrived only a minute or so after Harper changed Crystal into a simple pink dress and sun hat.

As she tucked Crystal into the stroller, Seth

said, "We can stroll around until five or so, then we need to get back to dress for dinner."

"It's formal?"

He shook his head. "No, but my mom is a stickler for time. She hates when anyone is late."

"Okay."

They rode the elevator to the lobby, which was filled with an abundance of flowers. The rich woods and marble gleamed in the afternoon sun.

Stepping out into the fresh air that smelled faintly of the rain that had fallen as they drove from the airport and onto gray brick streets, she inhaled deeply. The rich aromas of a nearby bakery teased her. "Makes me wish I hadn't eaten yet."

Seth slid on his sunglasses. Harper looked at him out of the corner of her eye. Not only did his life not revolve around money, but he also seemed so casual with her. As if walking the streets of one of the world's most wonderful cities with a widow and her baby was fun.

He turned to her, looking sexy and male in his leather jacket and shades. "Where to?"

"I don't know." She laughed lightly. "Let's just walk."

"If you only want to take a stroll, here's what

we'll do." They started down the street and made a turn that took them to Champs-Élysées.

She gasped. Leafy green trees and shops lined the gray brick-and-marble avenue, along with restaurants and vendors. The Arc de Triomphe stood like a sentinel at the end. Tourists bobbed and wove along the busy sidewalk.

"Because we're not going to be here long and most of our time will be spent at the gallery with Sabrina, I thought this might be the best way to see at least a little of Paris."

She inhaled again. "This is amazing."

"This is one of the best parts of Paris." He pointed at some shops. "You can buy anything from a cheap souvenir to a diamond tiara."

She gaped in awe. "I see that."

"Plus, it's the best place to get a real take on the people. On any day, you can walk into a designer store and see anybody from a rock star to a tourist who'd saved his whole life to get here."

She glanced around, still amazed. "I'd save to come back here." She shrugged. "Maybe see the whole city."

"Or sit at a sidewalk café and enjoy the show the tourists put on." He motioned to the right. "I haven't really had my morning quota of coffee. Do you mind if we stop? I'll buy you a croissant."

"I just ate!"

"Yeah, but sniff the air again."

She did and was rewarded by the scent of butter and vanilla, cocoa and coffee.

She groaned. "All right. I probably could eat a little something else."

They settled on seats at a round table in the corner of the café. Harper lifted Crystal from her stroller and set her on her lap as Seth ordered in French.

This time she didn't look at him as if he were special. She was finally beginning to realize that his life allowed him to ease himself into other cultures, other worlds, places she'd probably never see.

She glanced at the baby on her lap and sort of understood her mother's fanaticism with becoming wealthy. Except her mom only wanted to lunch with the right people. She didn't understand the lush, broad life having money could provide. She just wanted to look good in Chanel. She was missing everything.

The waiter brought a pot of coffee and a tray

of croissants and some things Harper didn't recognize. Her mouth watered.

Seth pointed to the tray. "These are madeleines, little cakes, and these are macaron." Glancing at her, he smiled. "My suggestion is take a bite of each."

That sounded like a good idea to her.

As he poured the coffee, she gingerly lifted one of the madeleines and bit into it. Her tongue rejoiced. "Oh, my God. There is no way I'm not eating this whole thing."

"Go ahead." He set a cup filled with coffee on the saucer beside her. "You're too thin, anyway."

And he'd noticed.

She shifted Crystal on her lap, took a sip of the rich, dark coffee, then finished the fluffy little cake that all but melted in her mouth.

Seth grabbed a croissant. He wasn't going to Paris and not eat a pastry. But he surreptitiously kept his eyes on Harper as she indulged in the treats. Not only did he mean what he'd said about her being too thin, but it also pleased him to watch her indulge.

Now that he knew she and Clark hadn't been on the solid financial ground that Seth had believed they were, he sincerely doubted anyone had ever spoiled her. Oh, her parents had given her things. Tons of things. All the things her image-conscious mother thought she should have. And Clark had given her things. All the things he needed for her to have to keep up the impression that he was financially stable.

But no one had ever spoiled her. His mission to show her a good time at the cocktail party had worked—until he'd flirted with her. So today he'd make it his mission to give her the best three days she ever had—without the flirting.

Crystal made a sound. Halfway between a "goo" and a "coo," the light noise floated over to him.

Seth tried to stay silent but couldn't. "Did she talk?"

Harper laughed. "No, she said 'goo.' I've been working with her."

"Working with her?"

"Getting a baby to say 'goo' is a way to get her acquainted with her vocal cords."

Seth never realized it was that complicated. His gaze stayed focused on Crystal. She looked at him and smiled before she pursed her little lips and said, "Goo."

He swore it was as if she knew he was curious. Mostly because she looked him right in the eye and seemed to say it to him.

His heart swelled. His throat tightened. It was so amazing to see a child learn that he was almost speechless from it.

Harper tickled her belly. "Are you chatty now?"

The baby giggled.

Seth sat mesmerized. Not because anything happening was so special but because it was so ordinary. He'd stayed away from babies all his life, thinking they were a nuisance or at least too fragile for him to be around. But Crystal wasn't. She was a little ball of cuteness.

He reached out and pulled her from Harper's lap. "Are you trying to flirt with me?"

When she giggled, he grinned. "Holy cow, she's cute."

CHAPTER EIGHT

HARPER STARED AT Seth as he held her baby at eye level and talked to her. Speechless didn't come close to what she was feeling. For a guy who'd only a few weeks before claimed he was afraid of babies, he held Crystal like a pro.

"You wouldn't be the first woman to try to steal me away."

Crystal patted his face. He didn't even blink.

Harper took a sip of coffee to ground herself in reality, but the delicious pastries were forgotten as he made stupid faces and talked with her little girl.

Warmth filled her, and she had to make a conscious effort not to let the amazing feelings she'd been having for weeks bubble up and form the word.

Love.

She could not love him.

She wasn't even supposed to like him, had struggled to keep her emotions in check. Yet here she was, with a feeling in the pit of her stomach that couldn't be denied. Love. Or at least the beginnings of it.

He was easy to be around, fun to be around, and he could no longer say he didn't like babies.

And she'd made her peace with Clark being gone.

She could love Seth. She simply couldn't do anything about it. He was a playboy, not the kind of guy to get serious. And even if he was...why would he pick her?

Clark's widow. She might be someone he'd play with, but that would be all.

Considering all these feelings were new, maybe they weren't fully formed? Maybe they were a possibility, not a total conclusion? Maybe she could guide them, so they wouldn't fully form?

She ended her debate with the knowledge that Seth was a great guy, worthy of her affection as a friend, and that settled her mind. It gave her great peace not to be fighting herself. She liked the idea of having feelings for him. She also liked the idea of controlling them. That was, after all, what adults did. Not let every little wisp in the wind drag them into things that were wrong for them.

That's how she could have a good time, not get hurt herself, not hurt or annoy Seth. Who probably wouldn't want to know she was feeling all this.

They spent the next hour with her pushing the stroller toward the Arc. But half the time Crystal wasn't in it. Seth picked her up and gave her her own personal tour of the city.

When Crystal tired, they went back to the hotel. Harper fed her and put her down for a nap, but she didn't go back to the sitting room with Seth. She took a long bath to pamper herself, then dressed for dinner early, knowing she had to take Crystal to the penthouse so the nanny Jake and Avery had hired could watch both babies.

She dressed Crystal in pajamas, then packed a diaper bag. When she came out of her room, Seth was nowhere in sight, so she left him a note that she was taking the baby upstairs to the nanny.

When she got to the penthouse, the luxury of it stole her breath. But Avery and Jake were so casual that she soon relaxed. She played a bit with Crystal, allowing little Abby to join a game of peekaboo, so both babies would be comfortable.

With the babies settled, they headed down in the elevator with Jake and Avery to get Seth because they were riding together to their mother's hotel for a predinner drink and then going to the restaurant.

Avery kept up a steady conversation with Maureen about projects the McCallans could support over the coming year, making dinner lively and even fun. Harper nearly volunteered to help with a campaign or two, but she kept her mouth shut. A month from now, she'd have a job. As a single mom, there was no guarantee she'd have time for projects.

The next morning, she and Seth ate breakfast in their suite and walked back to the café for lunch. Afterward, Seth played with Crystal while Harper dressed for the exhibit opening.

When she came out of her room, wearing a red sparkly dress that she'd picked up after her discussion with Avery about what to wear, Seth whistled. "See what a little croissant will do for you?"

She laughed. "I didn't gain weight overnight."

He handed her the baby. "You look amazing. Now, let me go get into my monkey suit and we'll be on our way."

"I'll take the baby up to the nanny."

Headed for his bedroom, he said, "Good idea."

Harper watched him go, feeling something she didn't want to describe. She'd settled this yesterday. Told herself it was okay to like him as a friend, a good friend, but it was wrong to fall in love. Though she couldn't deny the longing that rippled through her. She wouldn't let herself verbalize the wish that he'd fall in love with her. Knowing he didn't want a relationship with anyone was her one stronghold in reality. He might have gotten accustomed to her baby. He might even like Harper enough to flirt with her. But she'd never inspire in him the wish for anything beyond a one-night stand. She simply wasn't special enough. He was more the model, actress, rock goddess kind.

Two hours later they were hip-deep in a cocktail party. His sister, as always, dazzled in a blue dress that sparkled almost as much as her eyes did. In a city where her face wasn't instantly recognizable, she could easily be Sally McMillen for a couple of hours, mingle with fans and, in general, enjoy the fruits of her labors as an artist.

Still, she didn't hold a candle to Harper, who stood by Sabrina, in a circle of fans, listening to Sabrina talk.

Jake sidled up to him. "You know you don't have to eat dinner with us tonight."

He faced his brother. "What?"

"You and Harper could go somewhere alone. The nanny stays all night, so we could keep Crystal all night."

Not sure what his brother was hinting at, Seth stared at him. "What are you talking about?"

Jake nudged his shoulder. "You and Harper needing some time together. I see the way you're looking at her. Like somebody who doesn't get enough alone time." He leaned in closer. "Get a cab, take her to a restaurant with a view of the Seine. And be romantic."

Seth almost laughed. The last thing Harper wanted was for him to be romantic. She liked him as a friend. The nice guy who was helping her.

Although, he had decided that his mission this weekend would be to pamper her. A private dinner where she didn't have to listen to Sabrina's boyfriend Pierre whine, or worse, pout because Sabrina's work was getting more attention than his, would be a welcome treat. And not having to worry about getting up in the middle of the night would be even better.

His brother didn't have to know they weren't doing this for romance but to give her a weekend she'd remember.

"Thanks. I think we'll take you up on that."

He used his phone to find a good restaurant and his name to get a table. A half hour before the reservation, he walked up to Harper with the slim wrap she'd brought for the evening chill.

"What's this?"

"I've decided you've had enough McCallan time and I made reservations for dinner."

She blinked. "You did?"

He glanced around to make sure there was no one close enough to overhear. "Don't worry. Nothing romantic."

She blushed. "I didn't really mean that as horrible as it sounded."

He helped her with her wrap. "I get it. Clark and I were friends. No widow wants to date her husband's friend. Worse, I'm not exactly the guy who's going to settle down." He smiled. "We're both safe. But we're also both hungry and a little sick of Pierre. Let's go."

"Okay."

They tracked down Sabrina, his mom and Jake and Avery to bow out of dinner with the family and were on the street at the same time their car arrived. On the drive to the restaurant, she talked about sending out a few résumés the following week and before they knew it they had arrived.

A tall, slim man in a black suit led them to a quiet table in the back with a view of the lights sparkling off the Seine. A waiter had glasses of wine in their hands within minutes.

She took a sip, sighed and sat back on her seat. "You cannot believe how good this feels."

"Sure, I can. I've had long days at work and I imagine that's what being with my family has felt like to you. Work."

She shook her head, then took another sip of wine. "No. I like your family. A weekend with my mom would feel like work, but I've been having fun with your sister and Avery." She grew thoughtful. "I'm not sure how I lost my girlfriends. You get married and your life starts to revolve around a man and before you know it, his friends' wives are your friends." She shrugged. "When Clark was gone, those friends drifted away."

Seth leaned a little closer on the table. "Then they weren't very good friends."

"I suppose not."

She pointed out the window. "Look at the lights. It's amazing how the world can be the same yet different."

"Sort of like the difference between the beach and the mountains?"

"It's more than that. Paris is…warm. The people seem to enjoy feeding tourists."

He laughed. "You've obviously never been to Italy or you'd know the way Parisians treat you is not all that warm. I once went to a restaurant where the chef actually came out and sat with me because he knew I'd enjoy his new dish."

"No kidding." She smiled. "Where else have you been?"

He thought for a second. "I haven't been as many places as I'd like. My work has taken me all over Europe and I've even been to the Middle East and some of Asia but what I'd really like to see are places like Dubai."

"I'd like to see Scotland and Ireland."

"Really?"

"They just seem so green and lush."

"And you have a thing for taverns?"

She laughed. "Maybe."

Their food arrived, and she again ate with gusto. Their conversations went from travel to

Crystal to how grateful she was that he was selling her his condo. His mind clouded at the idea of her living in his condo without him. Luckily, by then their meal was long gone and their last glasses of wine had been finished.

Outside, he reached for his phone to call for a ride, but she stopped him. "Let's walk a bit."

The urge to take her hand rose in him, but he'd learned his lesson and kept his hands in his pockets. It was ironic that around his family, he could touch her as much as he wanted, but along the banks of the beautiful river, with the sensuous air of the romance of Paris surrounding them, he had to keep his distance.

Stars twinkled overhead. As the air began to chill, lovers huddled together, laughing, stealing kisses. But he and Harper walked along, quiet, not touching.

When she shivered, he said, "Okay. That's enough. It might be the most wonderful walk of your life, but I won't let you freeze to death."

He called for a car, then draped his suit jacket over her shoulders.

"You don't have to do that."

"I know." But he wanted to. Not because he wanted her evening to be special, perfect. Because everything in him warmed when he was around her. His life didn't seem work-driven. His family wasn't oppressive.

But she was the only woman who'd ever broken his heart. He wouldn't fall for her again. He wouldn't let himself.

The lights that winked off the Seine didn't have a thing on the glow inside of Harper. Standing without a suit coat, in his white shirt and bow tie, Seth looked like a picture from a magazine. She waited for him to say something, to step close and kiss her, but, of course, he didn't.

She'd told him not to.

They rode to the hotel in silence and stayed silent on the ride up in the elevator.

When he opened the door to their suite, she remembered that Crystal was staying the night with the nanny in Jake and Avery's suite and her breath stalled in her chest. His whole family believed they were sleeping together.

Maybe this was why Seth had let the romantic mood pass as they walked by the Seine? He didn't want her to get any ideas about how the night should end?

Or maybe this was her chance? She was the

one who'd told him no relationship. Because of Clark. Then she'd come to terms with Clark being gone, but she worried she wasn't the right woman for a man of the world.

The breath that had stalled in her chest burned in her lungs, as she stepped inside the suite. They were alone. But too many questions stood between them. Worse, the very fact that they were alone, in a suite, for the night meant she couldn't flirt or tease or even kiss him—even talk to him about her new thoughts about Clark—without looking like she wanted to seduce him.

There was no middle ground here. It was either friend or lover…temporary lover.

"Drink?"

She spun around too quickly and almost knocked herself off balance. "Um. No." She'd need her wits about her to get through this, and she already wasn't steady on her feet. Her whole body trembled with a combination of need and fear.

He took two crystal glasses from beneath the bar, anyway. "Are you sure? I know you had some wine with dinner, but you don't need to worry about waking up with Crystal. This might be your last chance for a long time."

She tried to smile. He was making a joke, but to her everything happening was deadly serious. Clark hadn't been her first, but there hadn't been many guys before him. Did she really want the first guy she slept with after her husband to be somebody guaranteed to break her heart?

"Maybe I will have something. More wine?"

He dipped down to reach below the bar again. "Coming right up."

She shrugged out of his jacket and laid it across the back of the sofa as he walked over with their drinks. He handed her the wine, then sat on the chair.

She frowned, feeling she'd gotten this situation all wrong. Oh, she still knew his whole family thought they were sleeping together. But he didn't seem to have any plans to seduce her.

"So, it was a good night?"

She nodded and sat on the sofa a few inches from his jacket, which still smelled like him and the air in Paris at night. Her heart lurched. Yearning spilled through her.

She whispered, "It was a really good night."

"I'm glad. I see how hard you work with Crystal. I know how hard your life is going to get."

She nodded. He wasn't making a move. He'd

either gotten beyond whatever it was he'd felt at the cocktail party, or he was waiting for her. Waiting for her to say she'd gotten beyond Clark and was ready.

For one night.

Because she wasn't sure he would give her more.

Hell, she wasn't even sure he wanted her now.

Confusion overwhelmed her. She bounced from the sofa. "You know what? I'm more tired than I thought. I think I will take advantage of this night without the baby and sleep."

She caught his gaze, looking for what, she wasn't sure. A sign that he wanted her. A word that this wouldn't just be a one-night thing for him.

He looked down at his drink. "Okay. Good night."

She sucked in air to stop her shivering chest. "Good night."

CHAPTER NINE

SETH DIDN'T KNOW why he'd been foolish enough to think things between him and Harper might be changing. He wasn't even sure why he wanted it. He wasn't the guy who believed in happily-ever-after...so what had he thought might happen that night?

Caught between frustration and confusion, he kept his distance for the rest of their trip and even after they returned home. Days were easy because he worked. Nights, he scheduled a few house showings with Bill Reynolds.

The following Saturday morning, he slept in and in the afternoon, he took the Ferrari to Montauk to see if there were any houses with For Sale signs that he could tell Bill about. But Saturday night, he had no choice but to shower and dress for the ball.

He waited until the last second to come out of his room, only to find Harper was nowhere around. He looked left and right and suddenly her bedroom door opened and she stepped out.

Wearing a pale pink strapless dress that caressed her top, slid down her waist and belled out in layers of tulle from her hips to the floor, she knocked him for a loop.

She touched the diamond teardrop earrings that looked oddly familiar to Seth. "Your mother let me borrow these."

"Oh." *When had she seen his mother?*

"If you don't like them, I can give them back."

"No. They look great. Beautiful." She looked beautiful. Elegant yet somehow elfin. Like a fairy you'd see in the mists of Ireland. He almost said that. Almost told her that she probably wanted to visit Ireland because she'd belong there. But he held his tongue.

She walked over to him and smiled. "I really don't want to go to this any more than you do."

He held the gaze of her soft blue eyes for a few seconds, then blinked and looked away. "I actually enjoy this ball."

"Oh, then it really is me."

He busied himself finding his keys.

"I know we decided on no relationship. But I

thought we were friends. We're supposed to be helping each other."

The slight tremble in her voice made him squeeze his eyes shut. All along his main goal had been not to hurt her, yet it seemed he had. Still, there was no way to avoid it. Just as he'd realized when he decided to sell her this condo, they had to untangle their lives, go their separate ways.

When he opened his eyes again, he grabbed his keys and slid them into his trouser pocket. "I've just been preoccupied."

"Looking at houses?"

"That and with work."

"Was I not doing a good job finding you somewhere to live? Because that's part of our deal, Seth. I help you find a house and you sell me your condo interest-free."

He turned from the kitchen island. "The truth is I realized this was going to be a bigger job than I'd thought. I don't want to take you away from the baby."

"That's not the deal. I only agreed to no interest on my loan for this place because I'm helping you find somewhere else to live. If you change that, I can't take the deal."

* * *

Pride made Harper stand taller. She realized that a relationship wasn't in the cards, but she wasn't a loser. She was a grown woman with a child who was entering the workforce. She and Seth had made an agreement and if he dropped his end of it, then the deal was dead. No matter how much it disappointed her to lose this condo, which was perfect for her and Crystal, she would not take charity.

Seth shook his head. "I get it. I'm sorry. I won't see another house or condo without you. I really didn't know how much work this would be. Or that I wouldn't like being locked out of the process."

She breathed a silent sigh of relief, but she saw what was going on. "I won't lock you out of the process."

"It just seemed that you and Bill were so tight that I worried you'd knock out things that might have been right for me."

Because she didn't know him. He didn't have to say it. The first few weeks they'd lived together they were close. Then they'd gotten a little too close and the past week they had been like two strangers living together. It was as if those first two days in Paris hadn't happened.

"Then maybe we need to go back to you coming along on all the viewings. I can sort through the listings on Bill's website, choose three or four and have you go with us when we see them."

Seth turned away. "Okay."

She got her wrap from her bedroom, so they could ride in the Ferrari with the top down, but it wasn't as much fun as it had been the night of the cocktail party. That night, she'd felt so free. Tonight, disappointment rattled through her. Not that she wanted him to be falling for her. She'd sorted that out in Paris.

It was just that the woman in her was so lonely, so miserable. So empty.

The first weeks they'd lived together he'd put light back into her life. Now he barely spoke to her.

They'd made the right choice. She knew they had. But the decision not to take things further had taken away their friendship and left a huge void, a hole in her heart.

A week ago, she would have included losing Clark as creating part of that hole. Now, she knew the truth. She was losing the first friend she'd made after losing Clark.

They entered the hotel hosting the ball the same way they'd entered the art museum for the first cocktail party they'd attended. The valet happily took Seth's car. A hotel employee cheerfully opened the doors for them. And Seth didn't even have to mention his name to get entry to the ball. Everybody knew him.

And maybe that was part of why she'd liked him so much. He was easy to be around, easy to laugh with. And she'd been alone for an entire year. She'd been vulnerable. Even if she hadn't realized it, she'd longed for somebody in her life.

With a fierceness that stole her breath, she suddenly missed being close to someone. She missed knowing somebody loved her. Missed having a place. Missed being somebody's love.

Seth's mom scurried over. "Our table is in front of the room."

Seth nodded. "We'll be up in a minute. There are a few people I want to introduce Harper to."

Maureen's eyebrows rose.

Seth laughed. "There are a lot of businesspeople here. Potential for Harper to find a job."

The jab burned through her. A reminder that she was nothing but a responsibility to him.

Because she was. Without a real relationship, she was nothing but a woman with a baby who desperately needed work. Not somebody he cared about. Not somebody he thought was beautiful. Or funny. Or nice to have around. A responsibility he was growing tired of.

They wove through the crowd with Seth saying hello to at least fifty percent of the people they passed. Then he stopped and introduced her to John Gardner, a banker.

Harper remembered walking down the hall with Bill Reynolds the first time they'd looked at condos, feeling like a businesswoman doing a job, and she channeled that confidence.

Standing a little taller, she extended her hand to shake John's. "It's a pleasure to meet you."

"Harper's reentering the workforce."

John's gaze flicked to hers. "Really. What kind of work are you looking for?"

"Assistant," she answered before Seth could. She'd leaned on him far too long. She could do this now. She had to. She *wanted* to. "In college, I ran a small business where I did odd jobs for people with more money than time."

Tall, gray-haired John snorted. "I get that. I have someone shop for the gifts I get my wife." He glanced around nervously as if realizing his wife could be close enough to hear him. When he saw she wasn't, he breathed a sigh of relief. "Can't let her know that, though."

Harper took the cue and assured him, "Confidentiality is the number one code of a good assistant."

"You better believe that." He glanced at his drink, then back at Harper. "And you think those skills will translate to an office?"

"Not in a traditional way," Harper admitted. "But wouldn't you rather have someone in your office who would find your last-minute gifts, as well as print the financials you have to review that afternoon?"

"I always had my assistant send my apology flowers."

Her confidence building, Harper said, "I'm also helping Seth find a new home right now. I'm looking at condos suggested by the real estate agent and weeding out the ones that are definite nos."

"That's a little above and beyond an assistant's job."

"True, but you never know what you're going to need from an assistant so it's good to have one who is versatile."

"So, what are you finding out there?"

"In the real estate market?"

John inclined his head.

"Are you considering moving?"

"My company is looking for an apartment for long-term visitors. It's okay to put someone up in a hotel when they are in town for a meeting or two. But when you have board members who are in town with their families or auditors or potential investors who'll be spending a week or ten days, it's better to have a condo they can use."

"I saw two a few weeks ago that Seth wasn't interested in. I can give you the name of our real estate agent and he can take you to see them."

"I'd rather have you stop by our office, talk with staff about what we're looking for and weed out all but three choices for us."

"Oh."

He pulled a card from his pocket. "My assistant's email is on there. Contact her Monday and we can arrange for you to come in for a meeting."

Happiness bubbled up from her chest and

she knew it spread all over her face. "Okay. Thank you."

John ambled off and Seth said, "And *that's* how you network."

She slapped the little business card against his biceps. "Come on. It was a coincidence that he was looking for a condo."

"You think?"

She laughed but stopped suddenly, the expression on his face bringing her up short. With his dark hair and dark eyes, his black tux gave him a sexy, mysterious look that sent her pulse scrambling. Plus, he was smiling at her. Warmly. The way he had the night she got the impression that he was attracted to her.

"Before you meet with him and his staff on Monday, we'll have to figure out a realistic amount you should charge for this service."

"What service? If they had someone who had time to meet with a real estate agent, they wouldn't need me to narrow their choices down for them."

"Exactly. The point is they don't have someone on staff who can take the time to look at condos. Thus, they hire you."

"So, I have a temp job?"

"No. You're a consultant. You have one of those rare opportunities where you can charge fifty or sixty thousand dollars for a few days' work."

She gaped at him. "Fifty or sixty thousand dollars!"

He grinned. "I know."

A tall red-haired man approached them.

Seth pivoted to face her. "This guy needs a full-time assistant. You'll get the extra cash from the real estate gig, but Max could actually hire you."

When the tall, red-haired man reached them, Seth took his hand and shook it. "Max Wilson. How have you been?"

"Great!" Max said, pumping Seth's hand.

Seth pointed to Harper. "This is my friend, Harper Hargraves."

"Hargraves? Related to Clark?"

Once again, she barely felt a twinge of sadness. She'd always miss Clark. Always have love for him in her heart. But she needed a job. This man needed an assistant. She couldn't blow this chance.

"Yes. He was my husband."

"I am so sorry for your loss. Hard to believe it's been a year."

"Yes. A year. That's why I'm out and about again. Even looking for a job."

Max asked, "What kind of work are you interested in?"

"I think I'm qualified to be an assistant."

His face brightened. "I'm losing my long-time assistant." He shook his head. "Feels funny to even think about hiring someone to replace her."

"I understand." She smiled at him. "I'm new at looking for a job. At university, I ran a virtual-assistant business. I bought flowers, walked dogs, bought gifts, sent reminders. I have a child now, so I want to shift those skills into a job that's more structured, so I can be home for dinner."

"That makes sense."

"But that doesn't mean I wouldn't enjoy the challenge of being someone's assistant. I had gotten to the point with some of my clients that I could anticipate what they needed. I kept logs of their friends' birthdays, anniversaries, that kind of thing, and kept them on track."

"Sounds a lot like what my assistant does." He took out his phone, scrolled to his schedule.

"If you're interested, I have an opening at ten o'clock on Monday morning. Which means you'd need to come in at nine to talk with Human Resources first."

"I'm definitely interested."

"Give me your number. In case the timing doesn't work for HR."

She rattled off the number for her cell phone and he put it in his phone. "If you don't hear from her you're good for Monday at nine."

She nodded, and Max walked away to talk to a couple across the room.

Harper pivoted to face Seth. "That was great."

Seth beamed at her. "It was because you were great. Now you've conquered your I-need-a-job nervousness, you are amazing."

He said it casually, but after the words were out of his mouth, his face changed. He blanked all emotion from it, almost as if he regretted calling her amazing.

Sadness echoed through her again. Not about Clark. About Seth. Knowing there would never ever be anything between them. After he found a house and she found a job, they might not even remain friends.

The thought brought her up short, stalled her

breath. If her interview worked out and Bill Reynolds came through with a house for Seth, this might be their last "date" together.

Cocktail hour ended with everyone taking seats for the dinner. They sat with Avery and Jake, Maureen and Sabrina and Pierre, who made dinner uncomfortable by complaining that nothing was up to his standards.

At the end of the meal, when he left to talk to a friend, Jake shook his head at Sabrina. "You need to dump that guy."

Seth said, "At the very least, send him back to France and forget his cell number."

Maureen said nothing, but her very silence confirmed she believed what everyone else did.

Luckily, dancing began. The band played a popular song and Jake rose to dance with Avery. Maureen gave Seth a significant look.

He glanced at Harper with a smile that was totally forced. "Would you like to dance?"

Harper almost refused. But Maureen sent her the kind of look that brooked no argument and Harper knew it would be near fatal to go against the McCallan matriarch.

"I'd love to."

By the time they got to the dance floor the

song had ended. A slower song began. Seth hesitated but slid one hand around her waist as he joined their hands.

The terrible sensation of dancing with someone who didn't want to be with her slithered through Harper at the same time she realized she was touching him. All those times her fingers had itched for it, she finally had her hand on his shoulder and her other hand held by his.

Her high heels brought them to eye level, but she didn't dare look at him while her hand was on the soft silk of his tux, making her blood shimmer through her. She tried not to notice his hand at her waist or that the distance between them seemed to shrink with every step, as if they were being drawn together by an unseen force.

She inched back and ruined their dance step.

"Relax."

"Easy for you to say. You've been to a trillion of these things."

"You came every year with Clark."

But she'd never felt these weird longings and curiosities with Clark. Of course, she'd always known Clark loved her. Maybe part of the yearning that coursed through her was simply an acknowledgment that Seth was unattainable?

Because she'd pushed him away.

"Clark and I did come to this ball every year."

"Do you miss him?"

For that she lifted her eyes until she caught Seth's gaze. "Not in the way that I did a few months ago."

She wasn't sure if it was her imagination, but she swore Seth's grip tightened on her waist.

"I'm sorry."

"Don't be. In the past few weeks, I've come to terms with the idea of moving on."

His head tilted. "Really?"

"Hey, I'm buying a condo, getting a job. I let go of the house that was our home. I've been alone for twelve long months. I was pregnant alone. Had a baby alone." She stopped, realizing she was about to tell him she was lonely. She hadn't been. The first two weeks she and Seth had lived together had been fun. So much fun.

"That must have been hard."

"It's amazing what you can do when you have no choice."

"Weren't your parents around?"

She shrugged. "They called a few times. Came to visit a lot in the beginning to make sure I was okay."

"They love you."

"In their own way."

"And your mom's not so bad." He shook his head. "Look, I know firsthand how difficult family can be, but I think you should give your mom a second chance."

She ignored his suggestion, mostly because it made sense and it shouldn't.

"Do you regret going to work for your family?"

"No. This is my responsibility. I accept it."

She frowned. "Then what are you doing that you have no choice about?"

He caught her gaze, looked like he might say something, but stopped.

But he didn't have to say it. He wanted away from her enough to give her his condo and almost let her choose his next home. "You're unhappy that you took me and Crystal in, aren't you?"

"No."

The word was a wisp. As soft as a cloud but as strong as good whiskey. She thought for a moment that he was too kind to let her believe she was a burden. But his eyes held hers, serious, sincere.

He regretted that they couldn't have something together.

* * *

At the end of the song, Seth walked Harper back to their table, sorry that he'd brought up Clark. Not because it filled her with sadness, but because it hadn't. And that conjured all kinds of notions in his head.

She finally seemed happy to be moving on. Of course, he knew no one wanted to be stuck in grief for the rest of their lives. Getting out of that emotional quagmire might have been what she was happy about...

But whatever the reason, she was moving on.

They went back to the table and she got hoodwinked into working the crowd with Sabrina. His sister was always on the hunt for mentors for the budding entrepreneurs in her program. But she'd reminded Harper that she could use all the contacts she could to help with her job search.

He watched them move through the crowd. Sabrina in her simple white gown, charming the rich and generous. Harper was shy at first, then she gained her confidence and worked the room in a different way. She might be softer than Sabrina, but she was no less determined to get a job.

To move on.

She was more than ready.

When they returned to the table, Seth asked Harper to dance again and though it took three songs, the band finally played something slow and romantic. This time when he took her into his arms, he felt her tense then relax. Every few steps, he'd bring her an inch or so closer until she was almost pressed up against him.

That's when he stopped. She hadn't protested. But his conscience reminded him that she was a kind, wonderful woman with a child. A widow. And he was a womanizer. No matter what anyone said about the right person changing a man's life, Seth knew his reasons for staying single, staying unattached, were deeper and more important than those of the usual playboy.

It might soothe his ego to think Harper liked him but, in the end, he would hurt her.

He moved away from her when the song ended. "Shall we go back to the table?"

"Yes."

Her voice sounded a little shaky. Which didn't surprise him because being near her had him a bit trembly, too. To get them both past their discomfort, he said, "I saw you having fun with Sabrina."

She turned to him with a laugh. "Fun? The woman's a dynamo! I got the cards of three more executives who are considering adding another assistant to their staffs. I'm going to be employed before the month is out."

"That's good."

"It's fantastic." She took a long breath. "You know, the part about losing Clark was devastating. But I never realized how much I had missed when I decided not to work after we were married. Makes me wonder what else I missed."

She started walking toward their table again, but her comment had stopped Seth dead in his tracks. *What else she'd missed?*

He could guess a hundred things she'd probably missed, most of them involving his king-size bed. And, oh, Lord. What he wouldn't give to be the guy who showed her.

He headed back to the table chastising himself.

But watching her laugh with his sister, he remembered what she had said about losing her friends. She also didn't have a sister. He saw a different side of her as she laughed with Sabrina. A girlie side. The side she probably didn't have time for because of the baby and, soon, work.

When they got in his car to go home and the

wind tousled her hair, sending her laughter to him on a wave of cool air, the conclusion he drew didn't surprise him.

This was a woman who was changing. She'd gone from devoted wife to single mom and would soon be an employee. And she wasn't sad about it. She'd finally found the fun in it.

What if she was done with the white-picket-fence dreams? Or what if she'd put them on hold until she'd experimented a little?

What if this was his one small chance, his one tiny opening, to have the woman he'd always wanted. Not forever. Not for always. But for a season of time as she experienced life?

If he let her go, found a new house, moved out and never saw her again, would he be depriving them both of an opportunity fate seemed to have handed them on a silver platter?

Or was he crazy to be thinking like this? Thinking she wanted him? Thinking they could have something to remember forever before they both moved on?

He parked the car and they rode up in the elevator in silence. He unlocked the condo door and motioned for her to enter before him. Mrs. P. mumbled a quick report on the baby and an even quicker goodbye before she shuffled out the door.

And then they were alone. She headed toward her room, but he caught up to her at the kitchen island, grabbed her hand and turned her to face him.

Her pretty pink skirt ruffled as she pivoted. Her eyes jumped to his.

He saw the surprise, but he also saw the curiosity before she could hide it. He thought of the kiss all those weeks ago in front of the limo, thought of her eager response, and kissed her again, before he could talk himself out of it.

CHAPTER TEN

THE KISS STARTED off slow and smooth but quickly went deep. Not a sweet, thanks-for-the-nice-evening kiss, but a prelude to making love. The kiss of a man who wanted a woman.

Excitement, fear and wonder coursed through Harper. His hands slid along the bare skin of her back, along the curve of her waist, and raced back up again as his mouth worked its magic. She pressed her fingers to his chest, wanting to slide them to his shoulders, but they paused, savored. Everything was so much more intense than it had been with Clark. She wondered if that was because they had been so young when they married, or if Seth was simply a different kind of man.

Just when she might have made a move to slide her hands beneath the sleek material of his tux jacket, he pulled away.

Her gaze leaped to his.

"We've already said you and I aren't a good mix."

His strong, sure voice made the statement with a confidence that confused her after the way he'd just kissed her.

"We want different things. But I sense things have changed since Paris. You've adjusted to the fact that you're starting a new phase of your life, and I think you might want to try some things you could have missed because you were so young when you got involved with Clark. I'm not the guy you settle down with, but I am the guy you could find yourself with." His eyes searched hers. "Think about that. No rush on the answer."

With that he turned and walked down the hall. She didn't move a muscle. She wasn't even sure she breathed until he opened the door and walked into his bedroom.

Then her breath poured out in a long, almost painful rush that drained her of oxygen and left her even more light-headed than his offer had.

And it was an offer. No-strings-attached sex. A chance to find herself.

After a year of loneliness, she'd been thrust into the eye of a storm of getting on her feet financially, finding a job and a home for herself and her baby, and now he was giving her a chance to find herself as a woman.

She understood what he meant. She was different than she'd been when she'd arrived on his doorstep. But it was the scariest proposition anyone had ever made to her. Not because she wasn't sure what it entailed, but because it tempted her in ways she'd never been tempted.

For that reason alone, she knew he was right. She did long to find herself, figure out who she was. But with him?

That was the variable. She absolutely knew she'd be someone different with him.

Was that why Seth was so tempting?

She walked back to her room, her gown swishing around her, the diamond earrings his mother had lent her swaying back and forth. She tried not to think of him, what he wanted, what he thought she should want.

She stepped into her bedroom. A pale nightlight illuminated the crib. Her baby. Her sleeping little girl.

She took off the earrings and laid them in the box Maureen had brought them in, then slid out of the fancy dress and tossed it across the room.

How could one little choice be so confusing?

* * *

Seth awoke feeling lazy and rested, then he remembered what he'd said to Harper the night before, remembered kissing her hungrily, remembered her greedy response…and that he'd propositioned her.

He pulled the covers over his head, then yanked them off again with a thump.

He'd never been ashamed of wanting a woman before. And she wanted him, too. She simply hadn't come to terms with it yet. But with time to think about it, maybe she'd changed her mind?

And if she hadn't, maybe he could help her with that?

He slid out of bed, found a pair of jeans and a T-shirt to slip into and headed out to the kitchen, his expectations teetering on the brink of believing she'd greet him with a smile, maybe a kiss—

When he got to the kitchen, she was feeding the baby.

Now what? He knew a kiss could get them over their morning-after awkwardness. And even with her sitting, he could walk up behind her, slide his arms around her and kiss the back of her neck, not giving her a chance to think about him or propositions or anything but the fact that they were attracted to each other.

Or he could just say "Good morning," and let her dictate what happened next?

She took the options out of his hands when she said, "Good morning," as he approached the kitchen island.

"Good morning."

Okay. That worked. But walking up behind her and kissing her neck was still a good follow-up.

She rose from the chair, set the empty baby bottle in the sink and wouldn't look at him as she turned toward the island again.

Suddenly, the neck kiss seemed highly inappropriate. Still, he could walk up to her, slide his hands along her arms and kiss her…

She was holding the baby. Nestling her against her chest.

Confusion confounded him. How did couples with babies kiss?

In their beds probably.

And he had yet to get her in his.

She wouldn't meet his gaze again and he knew he'd missed his chance to kiss her. He couldn't believe he was losing his suaveness.

He would get this. He was the king of smooth. He'd just have to switch strategies a bit.

She slipped past him. "I was thinking of visiting my parents today."

"Visiting your parents?"

She wouldn't look at him. "They don't see Crystal often."

He knew that. He just didn't realize she'd rather visit her mother than hang out with him.

"Today's supposed to be nice."

She'd rather visit her mother than hang out with him? "It is."

She motioned down the hall. "I'll just get us ready and be on our way."

"Okay."

"Okay."

He watched he walk to her bedroom, so desperate to get away from him that she was on her way to her parents' house.

At first, he wanted to kick himself for what he'd said to her the night before, then he realized a woman who didn't want anything to do with him would just tell him that. Quickly, like removing a bandage, she'd say "Forget it." But she couldn't tell him that because it would be a lie. So she was running.

His confidence returned. There might be a little thinking involved but he'd figure out how to woo her.

Having called for an Uber ride, Harper waited outside the building entry, talking with Hal, the Sunday doorman, who stood beside her holding Crystal's car seat. Close to seventy, he kept up a steady stream of light conversation, effectively keeping her mind off Seth until the car arrived.

He hurried over, opened the door and installed the car seat.

"Thanks, Hal." She was about to rummage in her purse for a tip, but he stopped her.

"It was just a car seat. And you're one of my favorite people." He smiled at Crystal. "Your baby is another."

His kindness released some of her tension. But not all of it. How did a woman say no to a man she really wanted? A man who'd looked like he wanted to kiss her that morning?

She had to stiffen to repress a shiver. She'd never experienced these emotions with Clark and though that made her feel a bit odd, it also revived her curiosity. Why were things always so intense with Seth?

No. "Things" weren't intense. They got along nicely until their attraction slithered into the room. Then her breathing changed. His eyes focused on her as if she were the only woman in the world. And the air disappeared from the room.

The driver began to chitchat and she had to reply. The light conversation eased Seth out of her brain and by the time she got into the elevator to her parents' enormous condo, she felt lighter.

No. Carrying her baby down the short hall to her mother's place, she felt like a single mom. Not a woman in a beautiful gown, wearing borrowed diamond earrings, being seduced by a man. Not a woman who wanted to throw caution to the wind, if only to satisfy her blazing curiosity. But herself. A woman with a baby who had to find a job, and who also needed a house. A woman with priorities that didn't include an affair.

A woman about to visit her parents with the baby they seldom saw because she was afraid they'd bring up all the wrong subjects.

She took a breath. Fortified herself.

She rang the bell and the maid answered, but her mom peeked out from behind the corner.

"The doorman said it was you." She smiled broadly and reached to take Crystal, as the maid took the car seat and tucked it in a convenient closet.

Glancing at her mom's taupe sheath, a nod to the fact that it was October, though fall temperatures hadn't yet arrived, Harper grimaced. "Be careful. I never know when she's going to throw up or pee."

Amelia laughed. "Diapers are stronger than they've ever been, and you threw up on me plenty." She headed for the elegant living room decorated in shades of sage, pale yellow and tan. "How are you today, sweet girl?" she asked Crystal as she tickled her tummy.

The baby giggled. Harper's dad rose from the sage sofa.

"What have we here? A rare Sunday visit?"

Harper kissed her dad's cheek, then gave the nonthreatening reply that would ease her out of having to give a real answer. "Bored today."

Her dad said, "Really? That's a good sign. For the past year, you've wanted nothing but to stay home."

Her mom sat on one of the tan chairs that complemented the sofa. "I agree. It's so nice to have you visit."

For the first time in about a decade, Harper relaxed with her parents. "Actually, it feels pretty good to get out of the house."

"And it's a lovely day," Amelia said, motioning to the huge wall of windows that displayed a panoramic view of Manhattan. "Maybe if you stay long enough we can take Crystal for a walk in the park?"

"I didn't bring her stroller. It was hard enough carrying her, a diaper bag and the car seat."

Her mother smiled. "Maybe next time."

Harper's muscles and bones loosened a little more. She glanced around, realizing that maybe her mother wasn't the crazy wannabe rich woman that she had been. In fact, she'd actually seen a bit of that change when her mom agreed to back off from dinner with her and Seth. "That'd be great."

Her dad said, "Can you stay for lunch?"

Harper's stomach growled. "I haven't even had breakfast. If you wanted to feed me now, I'd be overjoyed."

Amelia rose and handed the baby to Harper's

dad. "Let me talk to the maid. I'll bet she can have something ready in a half an hour."

"Wait." Harper rummaged through her diaper bag and pulled out the two just-in-case bottles she'd brought for the baby. "Can you put these in the refrigerator?"

"Absolutely."

When her mom was gone, Harper glanced at her dad. Crystal sat on his lap, patting his face. "She likes you."

"She should. I adore her."

Harper smiled, though her chest tightened. Her parents were a tad crazy, but a baby mitigated that. Or maybe Crystal brought out their softer side. Whatever the reason, this visit was going well, taking Harper's mind off Seth and into neutral territory.

"So, how's business?"

"Ridiculous," her dad said, with a sigh. "I can't keep up. I'll be hiring two new vice presidents in the next six months and the staff to go with them."

She almost asked if any one of those people he was hiring would need an assistant, but she stopped herself. Her parents' good, benevolent mood would die a needless death if she mentioned how desperately she needed a job.

Her mother sauntered into the room. "I'm back." She immediately took Crystal from her husband. "Brunch in thirty minutes."

"Thanks, Mom." It felt good to say that, good to mean it.

They chatted about Crystal until the maid came into the room and announced brunch was served. Harper was surprised to find her parents had a high chair with the proper padding and straps to balance a now four-month-old baby.

She ate eggs and toast, bacon and potatoes and topped it off with cheese blintzes and coffee. "I'm stuffed."

"I'm glad to see you eat." Her dad reached across the table and patted her hand. "You're so damned skinny."

Amelia brushed away his concern. "She's fashionably thin."

"I liked her better with a little meat on her bones."

Her mother sighed. "Seriously, Pete. You're so behind the times." She turned to Harper. "What does Seth think?"

The reminder of Seth stole all the air from Harper's lungs.

What did he think? That he'd like to sleep with her. Without a commitment. No strings attached. No tomorrow.

She said the only thing that came to mind. "We haven't gotten that far in our relationship."

Her mom gasped. "You haven't slept together?"

"Amelia!"

She glanced at her husband. "What? It's a perfectly normal question in today's world. Especially since Harper doesn't want to let him get away."

"Away from what, Mom?" And they were back to their old relationship. The one that made Harper crazy. "Should I get a rope and lasso him? Or maybe drag him to the justice of the peace and force him to put a ring on my finger when he doesn't want to?"

"I'm just saying…"

"Things aren't like what they were when you were young. Marriage isn't the first thing people consider when they date someone." The lie stuck on her tongue. Not because it was a lie but because nothing about what she had with Seth, what she felt for Seth, was normal. They weren't dating. But they were living together. When they'd begun living together, they hadn't been interested in each other romantically. Now...

Now...

She thought he was fun and smart and extremely generous.

But he only wanted to sleep with her.

She pulled her cell phone from her pocket and arranged for a car to pick her up.

Her mother's eyes dimmed with concern. "Honey, don't leave because I said something you don't like. I agree our generations are different about how we see life and especially relationships. I didn't mean to upset you or criticize what you have with Seth. Sit down. Have some more coffee."

"I'm fine. I need to get Crystal to bed anyway." And maybe face Seth. Tell him she was not made for what he wanted.

"It's just that you seemed to have had a totally different relationship with Clark. I recognize you were younger. But he pulled you away from us. Seth seems to be making you comfortable being around us."

Anger burst through her. "First of all, Clark did not pull me away from you." But he also didn't encourage her to visit. In fact, most times she'd planned to see her parents, he'd made bigger, better plans.

She sucked in a breath. Shook her head to clear it because she didn't want to think about that. Not now. Not today. Maybe not ever.

"Second, it wasn't Seth's idea for me to visit you today." But he had told her to give her mom a break, not be so hard on her. And he'd created the charade that they were dating to help Harper get through the situation that Clark had left them in.

Her mother rose from the table and began unbuckling Crystal's high-chair restraints. "You know what? We had a lovely visit today. And I don't want to ruin that by an offhand remark that rubbed you the wrong way. I love that you're dating Seth. I won't lie. But I love that you visited more."

"I liked the visit, too." She had. And she wasn't even angry with her mom. She was angry with herself because comparing Seth and Clark had her head spinning. Clark had been a great guy.

But he'd kept her from her parents and he'd left her broke.

All because he liked keeping up appearances, too.

Not wanting to sit around the house and mope, looking like a loser, Seth drove to Jake and Avery's house in Pennsylvania and dropped in on them unexpectedly. When he arrived at the huge house surrounded by trees, he could see the happy couple sitting on Adirondack chairs in the backyard near the pool. He drove his car up their long lane and walked across the lawn to greet them.

"Hey."

Jake set the paper he was reading on a convenient table and rose. "Hey! What brings you out here?"

Seth bent and kissed Avery's cheek. "I don't know."

"Where's Harper?"

"She left for the day. Visiting her parents."

And it was killing him. He'd never wanted a woman he couldn't have before. At least none that he remembered—

He frowned. Maybe he just had a really good

PR system in his brain that made him believe he was irresistible?

Or maybe those other women hadn't had babies that kept him from being able to kiss them?

Because he couldn't explain any of that to his happily married brother without telling him he wasn't really dating Harper, he said the first valid excuse that came to mind. "But I wanted to talk to Avery. I'm getting a new condo and I thought I'd get some insights."

Avery perked up. "Where are you looking?"

"Everywhere. I can't decide between a really lavish condo or a house in Connecticut."

Jake laughed. "A house in Connecticut?"

"I'm thirty-one. I live in a condo that I bought when I was twenty-six, just becoming successful. I want something…" He gestured broadly. "Something that says…"

Unable to figure out what to say, he left the sentence hang.

Avery motioned for him to take a seat. Jake headed toward the big deck. "I'll get some lemonade."

As soon as the sliding glass doors closed behind Jake, Avery turned to Seth. "Okay, now that he's gone, tell me what's really going on with Harper. Did you have a fight?"

"No. Sort of. A little one." And that was all he was saying. Honesty was one thing, but he would not tell his sister-in-law he wanted to sleep with Harper, not get into something permanent. That would spoil the charade, too.

"I really do need help figuring out what I want in a new place to live."

Avery inclined her head. "Tell me why you want to move."

"I want a home that's more me. Something that not the home of a guy just beginning to make it."

"And you'll need more of a home for a family?"

"No." His brain almost scrambled trying to keep up with what was real and what was a charade. He decided he might as well do with Avery what he'd done with his mom. Disabuse her of any happily-ever-after notions.

"Look, don't get too invested in me and Harper. You know my relationships don't last. I just want a nice home. A good place to have parties."

Though Avery's eyes filled with curiosity, she took the cue and didn't question him. "And you said lavish?"

He laughed. "You know what I'd like? A den. My condo is open floorplan so the TV's right there in the sitting room, which bumps up against the dining area. Everybody can see everything. I'd like a den."

"So that you could have a formal living room?"

"Yes. And a bigger master bedroom."

"Okay. How about the kitchen?"

"The kitchen could be nonexistent if it was only me. But I'll need a kitchen for a caterer."

"Okay. Big kitchen."

They discussed a few more details of what Seth wanted. Jake arrived with the lemonade and took his seat.

"So how far did we get in the discussion of Seth and Harper?"

Seth groaned.

Avery gave her husband a significant look. "You know it's against family rules to be pushy about relationships. And speaking of that, you shouldn't have said anything about Pierre last night at dinner."

"He's a tool."

"And Sabrina loves him."

"I don't think she does," Jake said. "I think he

pushed his way into her life and she just got accustomed to him."

Avery frowned. "Hmm. Now that you mention it, he was different in the beginning. *Pushy* might actually be the word for it."

"*Pushy* is exactly the word for it," Seth said.

The subject of Pierre died, and they drank their lemonade and talked about things Seth should look for in a new home. Twenty minutes later the baby monitor beside Avery squawked with the sounds of their one-year-old daughter, Abby, waking from her nap.

"I better go get her."

Avery raced into the house and Jake sat back on his seat. "So, what's really going on with Harper?"

Seth cut his brother a look. He had the same feeling he'd gotten the last time Jake had asked him about Harper, and it seemed wrong to be less than honest with him. He might not be able to discuss the ruse, but that wasn't his only problem with Harper. "I told her last night I wanted to sleep with her."

Jake winced. "You're not sleeping together?"

"In the beginning we were reluctant because Clark and I had been friends. But now, things are different. She's different. I think we should have an affair."

"And she wants to get married?"

"I'm not sure. But she knows I don't." He almost cursed. He hated talking about this kind of stuff. Even with Jake. "It's not like people don't have affairs. You had your share of them."

"True."

"And it's not like I didn't give fair warning, so she has time to think about it. We both have time to make sure it's the right thing. After all, she was Clark's wife." A wave of guilt hit him. The remorse about Clark that he'd felt before.

He groaned. "I'm paying back my debt to Clark by wanting to sleep with his wife."

"She's not his wife anymore," Jake said gently. "Seth, Clark is gone. And this might turn into something."

"It won't." He ran his hand down his face. He was tempting Clark's widow with an affair. Not marriage. Not even a relationship. Just an affair. Guilt rose in another warm wave. "You know how I am. I'm not the guy who's going to settle down like you did."

"How do you know?"

"A million things. Mostly Mom and Dad's

sham of a marriage." He shook his head. "It all seems like a trap to me. A prison. I'll never shake that. I can tell the minute a woman begins thinking about something permanent with me, and I run. Eventually I'd run from Harper, too."

"Then I think you need to send your real estate agent the list of things you want in a house and tell him to get a move on. You liked Clark too much to hurt Harper."

"Exactly."

Avery walked out holding Abby and the little girl nestled her face into her mom's neck when she saw Seth.

As Jake pulled the baby from Avery's arms, he leaned in for a quick kiss with Avery.

Seth watched in amazement. The trick to kissing a woman with a child seemed to be taking control of the baby.

"What's this?" Jake tickled Abby's tummy. "Are you shy with Uncle Seth?"

She buried herself even deeper into Jake's shoulder.

Seth shook off his thoughts about kissing a woman with a baby because he didn't need them now that he had his thoughts about Harper straightened out. He looked at his niece with new affection since Crystal had taught him how to be around a child.

"I can't believe how big she is."

"One year," Avery said proudly. She sidled up beside Jake, slid her arm around his waist.

Seth saw that too. Even a one-year-old didn't get in the way of her and Jake being affectionate.

"We're thinking about having another baby."

"Or six," Jake said casually.

Seth almost choked. His stiff and stoic brother wasn't merely casually affectionate with the woman he'd *married*. Now, he was thinking about having six kids? "You kind of hinted that in Paris."

Jake, a guy who had lived and breathed the McCallan legacy, finally had a life. A real life. And was happy. Though the temptation to tease him rose up in Seth, he couldn't tease about that. Not today.

Abby pulled away from her dad and looked at Seth. With her dark hair, round face and happy green eyes, she was the perfect combination of her parents.

"Hey, Abby."

She frowned.

"Come on. You can't be afraid of me. I'm

Uncle Seth. I'm the one who will buy you the best birthday presents."

Abby's brow wrinkled.

Seth laughed. "I'm willing to wait until you're five for you to like me."

He reached out and kissed Avery's cheek, chucked Abby's chin and said, "Okay, I'm off. I'll see you tomorrow, bro."

Jake said, "Unless you're meeting with your real estate agent."

"Right."

The three-hour drive home gave Seth plenty of time to call Bill and talk in detail about what he wanted in his new condo. Always eager to please, Bill told him he would dig a little deeper and, satisfied, Seth disconnected the call.

He stopped at a nearby restaurant and picked up Chinese for supper.

Obviously glad for the food, Harper said, "Great," as he arrived with the bags.

But there was an elephant in the room between them. She hadn't answered his proposition. And despite his conversation with his brother, Seth still wanted her to say yes.

They sat at the table. Both dished out their food.

"Where's Crystal?"

"Sleeping."

"I went to see my niece today." Instead, he'd noticed at least two ways men and women could touch and kiss around a child.

Surprised, she glanced up at him. "You did?"

"Actually, I was talking with Avery about what I'd want in a condo and Abby woke from her nap."

Harper didn't say anything, and Seth realized his mistake. Harper was supposed to be helping him find a new home. "It isn't that I don't trust your judgment. It was more that I had no idea myself what I wanted. She helped drag some things out of me."

She ran her chopsticks through her food, playing with it more than eating it. Seth almost groaned.

Would he ever get anything right with this woman?

"What kind of things did she drag out of you?"

"A den, for one. A separate room for the TV and the sitting area. A bigger kitchen. A master that's more like a suite."

The hurt in her voice lessened. "That's all good."

"I called Bill. He's on the hunt for a few new places and he'll be calling you tomorrow."

She brightened a bit. "Good. I also have that interview tomorrow."

That's right. Max really had seemed interested. "And you have to call John Gardner about the condo for his company."

"I thought I'd call him first, maybe set a time for the afternoon with his people while I'm still dressed for the interview."

Seth laughed. "Good thinking."

And just like that, they were friends again. Seth would have breathed a sigh of relief except something about them easily being able to forgive and forget settled into his gut. A feeling he'd never felt before. Not relief. Not exactly contentment. Something rich and right and totally foreign.

He'd had girlfriends. He had tons of friends. He had a brother and sister he was now close to. But this was different. This was special.

He told himself that was ridiculous, then watched a playoff game with her to prove to himself they could still be friends.

When it was time for bed, as they walked down the hall to their respective rooms, he remembered kissing her the night before, but to-night he didn't stop. He reminded himself that Clark had been his friend and if he really wanted to thank him for helping him get on his feet, he wouldn't hurt Harper.

No matter how flipping much he wanted to kiss her.

And now he knew how—take control of the baby.

He raced to his room. He would not hurt her, not kiss her and certainly not proposition her again.

CHAPTER ELEVEN

HARPER FELT FUNNY the next morning.

As Seth got coffee and she prepared a bottle for Crystal, the atmosphere of the kitchen was strange. If only being friends was the right thing to do, why did everything feel so off?

They didn't fight, weren't overly polite...but what had been ordinary and acceptable in the beginning of her living with him was now odd. Especially when he kept glancing at Crystal, looking like he wanted to say something or do something.

She supposed that might be because he'd seen his niece the day before. Maybe he'd gotten comfortable. Several times, it seemed like he wanted to pick her up, but changed his mind.

He'd held Crystal in Paris. Walked along the Champs-Élysées holding her, giving her a baby tour of the city.

Why did he hesitate now?

Seth left for work early—seven o'clock instead

of eight or nine. Harper dressed for her interview and at eight o'clock called John Gardner's office and set up an appointment for one o'clock with his assistant to discuss Harper helping them find a company condo. Then she left Crystal with Mrs. Petrillo and went to her interview.

On the walk to Midtown, she realized she could have left Crystal with her mom. Her mother would have loved that. The thought seemed to come out of nowhere, but it felt more right than the atmosphere in Seth's home that morning. She pushed those thoughts out of her brain and put her mind on possible interview questions as she finished the walk to Max Wilson's office.

The interview took two hours. She reported to his Human Resources department as Max had instructed and after twenty minutes of conversation she was given two tests. Then she was whisked to Max's office, where he made what seemed to be small talk, but actually delved into her life and the time she'd spent running her small business.

They shook hands and he promised he'd call before the week was out to let her know if she was a candidate for the job.

Though he hadn't hired her, he also hadn't said,

"Thanks but no thanks." She left his office feeling great. So great, that when her phone rang, she answered with a perky "Hello!"

"Hey. It's Bill. I'm guessing Seth told you we'd talked, and he added a laundry list of things he wanted in his new house."

"Yes."

"He said to call and let you know when I had something, and I have two things. One we'll have to look at this afternoon, though. The owners are eager to sell. It's not going to last."

"I can meet you around three."

"Do you want to call Seth?"

She thought about how weird he'd been about her looking at houses alone and decided she should ask him to come along.

"Yes. I'll call him. I know it's short notice but if he can't make it, I'll see it alone. If he can make it, he might be able to decide today."

Bill laughed. "He might have to."

"Okay. I'll call him now and let you know."

She headed for a nearby coffee shop. Not only did she have time to kill, but she was also hungry. Her dad's comment about her being too thin echoed in her head, backing up something similar Seth had said in Paris, so she bought a premade sandwich and Danish pastry to go with her coffee. A far cry from the pastries she'd had in Paris. But this was her life now.

She found a seat and called Seth. "Bill has a condo he thinks is perfect for you but it's also going to go quickly. He said you'll have to see it today."

"This afternoon?"

"Yes. I'm to call him with a time. I won't be out of John Gardner's office before three, so what if we tell him three thirty?"

"Sounds good."

"Okay. I'll call him then text you the address."

She disconnected the call and ate her lunch. With food in her stomach and a great interview under her belt, she walked into John Gardner's office a confident woman. She explained to John and his staff that she'd been looking for condos with Seth, had a real estate agent she was working with and she would happily be the person who takes the first look at potential condos for them.

John asked for her fee. She gave him the number Seth suggested and within what felt like ten minutes, she was hired.

Shell-shocked, she walked out of the building

and onto the sidewalk. With the money in her account from the sale of her and Clark's condo and the down payment on her services being wired in by John Gardner's company, she could afford a cab to get to the condo Bill wanted her to see.

She called for an Uber car. Now that she had more than a little bit of cash, she wouldn't be foolish...

Not that she'd thought Clark had been foolish.

She shook her head to clear those thoughts, got into the Uber car when it arrived and headed for the condo Bill wanted to show Seth.

As soon as she turned from paying the driver, she saw Seth standing just inside the double-door entrance, his hands in the pockets of his black leather jacket.

Her breath stalled at how gorgeous he was. His dark hair was just a little mussed, probably from a ride in his convertible. His dark eyes narrowed as he looked for her. When he saw her, his lips lifted into a warm smile.

Her heart flipped again.

She couldn't stop the tingles that coursed through her when she entered the lobby and he caught her hand. "You look fantastic."

She did a quick turn to show off her new outfit. A navy blue blazer over an orange flowered sheath and heels. It felt so good to be in heels again.

"It's amazing what new clothes will do for someone."

But she knew it was more than that. It had to be. She never felt more alive than when she was with Seth. Or more confused. How could she be happy around someone who seemed to be the exact opposite of the man she should love. Someone who didn't want what she wanted?

They told the doorman they were there to look at a condo with Bill Reynolds and he smiled. "Penthouse."

Harper and Seth exchanged a glance. "If that's the one Bill's showing today, then I guess we're going to the penthouse."

The doorman took them to a hidden, private elevator, and used a key card to set the car in motion. They rode in silence for what seemed like forever, then the doors opened on a huge great room with a wall of windows that displayed a view of Manhattan that looked close enough to touch.

She stepped out of the elevator. "Oh, my God."

Seth walked out behind her. "Wow."

The owner must have already moved because the place was empty. Shiny white marble floors winked at them.

Seth turned to the right and then the left. "I don't see a chandelier for the dining room or a kitchen."

"That's because they are separate rooms." Bill walked toward them, hand extended.

Seth shook it. "*This* is the living room?"

"Can you imagine having a party here?" Bill said, gesturing around the room. "Plenty of room for guests. But just think of that view at night. The lights of the city glowing from tall buildings. The moon hovering over them."

Harper could picture it. "It's so gorgeous," she said reverently.

Bill gestured to the left. "Let's take a look at the kitchen."

They followed him to a door that opened onto a butler's pantry with white cabinets and plenty of counter space to be a staging area for serving dinner, then into an all-white kitchen with stainless-steel, restaurant-grade appliances.

Harper walked from one appliance to the next, checking things out, and realized everything was new. "I'd get lost in here." She laughed. "It's huge. And everything's just been replaced. Why remodel and move?"

Bill shrugged. "Markets fall. Fortunes change. What this couple thought they could afford in January is now way out of their budget. If this thing sells today, they get a stake for a second chance."

Harper certainly understood that.

Bill showed them the dining room across from the butler's pantry, another room with spectacular views of the city. Two guest suites had the view on the other side of the building and the master suite—a sitting room, bedroom, dressing room, two closets and a bathroom the size of Seth's current kitchen—had yet another view of the city.

When they had gone through the entire place, Seth said simply, "I want it."

"There are two other bids."

"Do you know what they are?"

Bill frowned. "Sorry. No."

"Then let's come in at one-point-five million over asking."

Bill's mouth fell open.

Harper gasped. "Seth, that's a lot of money."

* * *

Seth didn't hesitate. He faced Harper. "When I see something I want, I go after it."

She gave him a curious look and he knew what she was thinking. He'd told her he wanted her, but after his talk with Jake, he'd backed off.

He might seem like a hypocrite to her, or a gentleman. He had no idea, and he also didn't care to find out. Things were better with them as friends, not even considering becoming lovers.

Even if he wasn't accustomed to walking away from things he wanted.

Oblivious, Bill said, "Let me call in your offer."

"Great. I'll call my bank."

Halfway through dialing, Bill stopped. "Are you telling me this is a cash offer?"

"Yes."

Bill grinned. "I think you just shot yourself to the head of the line. I'll need a cashier's check for a down payment to hold it."

The previous owners had left behind a desk, desk chair and two tufted chairs in the office. Seth excused himself to go into that room to call his banker. He made the arrangements, including having the check taken to Bill's office by courier, then he and Harper walked to his Ferrari.

"I hope you get it."

He opened the car door for Harper, realizing they were close again. Not just physically but emotionally. They were both thrilled that he'd found a home and if there was anybody he'd want to celebrate with, it would be her.

"I do, too."

"I've never seen views like that."

He scoffed, glad they'd found a safe topic of conversation. "Not even at your mother's?"

"No. And if she sees yours she's going to be house hunting again."

The second the words were out of her mouth, she shook her head, as if she regretted saying them.

Seth waited and finally she said, "I enjoyed my visit with my parents yesterday." She peeked across the car at him. "They loved seeing Crystal."

As much as she didn't want to admit it, she needed her parents, her family. Amelia Sloan might be a bit of an oddball, but Seth would bet with a few ground rules she'd be a good mother and a wonderful grandmother.

"That's great."

"It was."

Her voice had an unexpectedly wistful quality to it that made Seth want to ask questions, but he held back. Two years ago, when his father died, and Jake wanted him to work for McCallan, Inc., he'd agreed only to help his brother. But he'd worried about his relationship with his mom. Two years after his father's death, it felt odd still punishing his mother.

But it felt even odder thinking about getting warm and fuzzy with her.

When they arrived at his condo—soon to be Harper's if his offer went through—Mrs. Petrillo was watching a soap with Crystal happily sitting on her lap.

Harper needed to get out of her clothes, so she immediately walked back the hall to her room.

Seth debated a second, before he pulled Crystal from Mrs. Petrillo's lap. Not as a slick way to kiss Harper. She wasn't even around. Just as a way to hold her.

"I've missed you since Paris, kid."

Crystal giggled, then cooed. No prompting. No nothing.

"I think she likes me."

Mrs. Petrillo batted a hand. "She's been doing

that all day. Laughing at nothing. Happiest baby I've ever seen."

She headed for the door.

"Don't you want to finish your soap?"

"No. Andrea annoys me. And she's on today. If there's one thing I know about soaps, it's that when a character starts off the episode, most of the scenes will have her in it. I'm going to make a sandwich, then get ready for bridge."

"Your friends coming to your house tonight?"

"We're meeting at a coffee shop." She grinned. "Something different. Old people usually don't like change, so my group deliberately shakes things up." She pointed a finger at Seth. "That's how you stay young."

Seth laughed as she walked out the door and when it closed behind her, he sat on the sofa, settling Crystal on his lap. "So, how are you today?"

He remembered Jake tickling Abby's tummy, so he tickled Crystal's belly.

When she laughed, he smiled.

That's how Harper found them. Crystal on Seth's lap, looking up at him with adoring eyes and Seth smiling.

"I'll take her."

Seth batted a hand. "No. No. She's fine. Besides, I thought I'd let you choose dinner tonight from the takeout menus. We have a lot to celebrate."

Harper only stared at him. She knew he'd made friends with Crystal in Paris, but it was more the look he was giving her baby girl that tripped something in Harper's heart. *He liked her.* Maybe he'd even grown attached to her.

She meandered to the drawer with the menus. "Is there anything a man who is celebrating likes to get for dinner?"

"I'll tell you what we should do. There's a steakhouse a few blocks from here that will deliver if I promise a two-hundred-dollar tip."

She laughed.

"I'm serious. And they have a wine list to die for."

"You want to get steak and wine?"

"And maybe some fries and a nice salad." He paused. "Actually, my mouth is now watering." He rose from the sofa, strolled over to her and handed Crystal to her. "Let me call."

The food arrived an hour later. The delivery man all but set the table for them and Seth generously tipped him, as promised. He pulled the cork from the wine and poured.

Harper had just put Crystal to bed. The room was quiet. There was no baby carrier on a chair or the table.

"This is nice." She hadn't meant to make the comment, but she couldn't take it back because it was true. It was nice.

She almost took a sip of wine, but instead held out her glass. "A toast. To you getting the most beautiful condo I've ever seen."

He clinked her glass. "I hope. I hadn't realized how ready I was to move or how much my life had changed. But it's time."

"And I benefit."

"Yes, you do." He met her gaze. "I never would have done this without you."

She snickered. "You needed someone to take your condo before you could get another?"

"No. I don't like to do things like look at houses. I have a hard time with salespeople."

She smiled at him. "It was my pleasure to help you. I would have done it for nothing."

"Don't sell yourself short."

"I don't."

"You do. You're a smart woman who is going

to get an entry-level job and work her way up the corporate ladder."

She shook her head. "How do you know?"

"Because you have talent and ambition. I told you, I remember how hard you worked when you had the assistant company. Even then I thought the sky was the limit for you."

Warmth coursed through her, along with happiness. "I do have a baby to support."

"And you're a great mom." He held out his wineglass again. "Let's toast that. It's not easy being a working mom, but you'll do it."

"I will." Happiness glowed inside her. She couldn't remember ever feeling this good. She had a baby she loved, a condo soon to be hers, a consulting job that would pay her about a year's salary and she'd aced an interview.

She finished her wine and he filled her glass again as she picked up her knife and cut a piece of steak. When she tasted it, she groaned. "This is amazing."

"Aren't you glad I'm a nice enough guy that everyone's willing to deliver to me?"

"I am."

"So, tell me about the interview."

She told him about meeting with Human Resources first, then taking two tests, then talking to Max. He listened intently, didn't interrupt, didn't interject.

"He said he'd call either way. If got the job or didn't."

"He's a good man."

Harper turned thoughtful. "He really seems to be."

"He was one of the companies that refused to do business with my dad."

Because that was the last thing Harper expected to hear, she needed a minute for it to sink in.

"You like him because he wouldn't do business with your dad?"

"In a way, yeah." He set his fork down. "Max not even considering doing business with our company gave Jake the feeling he could have an ally when he eased our dad out of the chairman position for our board."

"Jake eased your dad out of his company's chairman position? I never heard any of this. Not even as gossip from Clark."

"Jake went behind the scenes to figure things out about McCallan, Inc. Our dad had been cheating subcontractors out of money, lying, fudging bids, that kind of thing, and Jake couldn't handle it. He got enough allies on the board to have someone else appointed chairman. Max became one of Jake's mentors. Which helped him when our dad died unexpectedly a few years ago. Our company now is nothing like what it was when Dad ran it. In a way, we have Max to thank for that."

"Wow." She almost couldn't believe what he had told her. But then again, she'd known there were reasons beyond rich-kid rebellion that Seth had left his family.

"I think you'd fit very well into Max's organization. You're honest and kind. You've won over our doormen and Mrs. Petrillo without blinking an eye."

She felt her face redden. "That was pretty easy. They're all nice people."

"See? Only a really kind person deflects praise."

She rolled her eyes. "Whatever." But she had to admit the fact that he thought her kind gave her another confidence boost. That and the way he felt she'd fit into Max Wilson's organization.

She almost told him about her mom, about the thoughts she'd been having the past couple of days. That it was time to make up, but she wasn't sure how.

But the baby fussed, and when she went to her room to check on her, she couldn't get her back to sleep. Her eyes were red-rimmed from crying, her cheeks wet with tears.

She carried her out to the living room, where Seth sat watching a baseball game.

When he saw her, he said, "What happened?"

"I don't know. Could be any one of a number of things. I think I need to call the pediatrician."

"Give her to me so you can talk."

He took Crystal and settled her on his lap, but as soon as Harper started talking, she began to cry.

Seth got up from the sofa and walked with her, talking soothingly as he approached the windows at the back of the sitting area. He pulled open the drapes, showed Crystal the lights beyond the glass, and she stopped crying.

Harper stared at him at them, her heart aching. Whether he knew it or not, someday he'd make a great dad.

She watched them for a few minutes as she waited for the pediatrician to come to the phone. When he came on the line, he listened to Harper's explanation and suggested that Crystal was probably getting her first tooth. He told Harper to examine her gums, see if she could feel a bump or see any redness and to apply an over-the-counter gel.

As soon as she disconnected the call, Seth turned from the window. "What did he say?"

"That she's probably teething, I should look for signs of it and use an over-the-counter teething gel."

"Can we get it locally?"

"I already have it. Teething can start as early as three months, so I bought some for when her teeth began to come in."

"Smart."

She walked over to take Crystal from him. "I just know to be prepared."

They set the baby in her carrier and Harper looked at her gums. "They're red."

She swiped a finger along the space that seemed the deepest shade of red and felt the bump.

"Yep. This is it. She's getting a tooth."

"Did you hear that, Crystal? This time next week, you can be eating steak with me and your mom."

She laughed, then sniffled.

Harper rose. "Stand by the carrier while I get the gel."

She raced into her room, found the gel and was back in a few seconds. She smoothed it across Crystal's gums then rocked her until she fell asleep.

After taking the baby to her crib, she walked out to the sitting area and plopped down on the couch. "This might turn into a long night."

"Might?" He laughed. "I think you could be up every twenty minutes."

She turned her head along the back of the couch to look at him. "Unless the gel works."

He nodded. "Unless the gel works."

She couldn't get over how comfortable he was, not just with Crystal but with the teething. "The first night I stayed here, you woke up when she cried."

He shrugged. "I was a newbie."

"You were."

"Now I'm a pro."

"Not a pro but close."

He got up from the sofa and went to the kitchen, where he grabbed a beer. "I'd offer you one, but I take it you're on duty."

"I know. I'm glad I didn't drink that second glass of wine."

He ambled back to the sofa. "So, what are you going to do? Sit up all night and be available for when she cries?"

"Maybe."

"Seriously?"

"This my first baby. My first new tooth."

He laughed. "I won't drink this beer and I'll take a shift."

She gaped at him. "Don't be silly. You have work in the morning."

"I know. But I feel like I should help."

"We'll be fine."

But he put the beer back in the fridge. The TV still played softly in the background with the sounds of the baseball game turned down low enough that that didn't interfere, but when someone hit a home run and the crowd erupted with a shout, Seth looked at the screen.

"They're winning."

"They are."

"Clark loved the Yankees."

Harper nodded.

They were quiet for a few seconds, then Seth

quietly said, "Ever feel bad that he's missing out on all these things with Crystal?"

She shook her head. "I should but I don't." She took a long breath, wondering what to say, what to hold back, and in the end she decided to be honest. "I don't think he'd have helped much with Crystal." She sneaked a quick peek at Seth. "Don't get me wrong. He wanted her. He wanted a family. But he'd have been more of an observer in her baby years. Happy to wait until she was old enough to throw a baseball or ride a bike before he got involved."

Seth looked shocked. "Really?"

"Yeah."

"But she's so funny."

"He'd have been able to resist her cuteness." She paused again. Bit her tongue once, but couldn't stop herself. She said, "He was more interested in business. I think he saw his place as being the one to provide the income and me the one to make the home."

"Sounds dangerously like my dad."

"Clark wouldn't cheat subcontractors."

"I know that. I'm sorry. It's just that my dad left all the home stuff to my mother, too."

The truth burned on her tongue. Not that Clark

was bad, but that she was angry. Seriously angry that he hadn't involved her on decisions that had affected her future.

She felt herself losing the battle, knew she couldn't hold back anymore. "Do you know my name wasn't on our condo?"

He peered over at her. "Clark didn't put your name on the deed?"

"After I found the huge mortgage on the condo, I understood that he hadn't put my name on, so he could use it as an asset."

Seth's mouth opened then closed. After a long sigh, he said, "I'm not going to tell you that's normal because I think you know it isn't."

"He did a lot of weird things. More than juggling our money and assets. Things like scheduling things on the same day I had planned to visit my parents or the same day my parents were having a party." She sucked in a long breath, not quite disgusted with herself for talking about Clark, but not about to stop, either. "I don't think he kept me away from my parents for any reason other than he knew we didn't get along. In his own way, I think he was protecting me."

"Maybe he was."

"*You* don't do things like that, though. You

don't tell me where to go or what to do. You've almost been a supporter of my parents."

He glanced at her, one eyebrow raised. "I'm the one who thought of the charade."

"Yeah, but you also say things like my mom's not so bad or she needs to see the baby." She pressed her lips together, then blew out a long breath. "I don't know where I'm going with this except that I had to talk to someone. Explain how I feel so I don't let my thinking go too far." She took another breath for courage before she said, "The month before I moved in here I stopped making excuses for Clark and started seeing him as a normal guy."

Seth didn't seem impressed. "We're all normal guys."

"I think all those months I stayed at home after Clark died, I was trying to hold onto the fairy tale. I didn't want to tell my mom Clark had failed because I didn't want to face it, either. I wanted to pretend everything was fine, even as my life was falling apart around me because of decisions he'd made."

"It's pretty difficult for a knight in shining armor to stay perched on a white horse his whole life."

She laughed. "I know. And I'm not angry with him. It just feels weird to settle into the knowledge that my husband wasn't perfect. That he had some pretty big faults. And he lied to me. Maybe not straight-out lied, but he didn't put my name on our condo, got a mortgage, leveraged the firm I thought was a cash cow."

"I understand. Try finding out your dad has a mistress…has had several mistresses. Kids think their dads walk on water. When I found out my dad was supporting a woman across town I was shell-shocked."

"That is bad."

"It gets worse. He never hit us, but he was a mean, spiteful person. He loved being in charge. He loved making people squirm. Even me and Jake." He shook his head. "Especially me and Jake. When we finally figured that out, we were at university, both broke, both jobless and soon-to-be out of our dorms because our dad hadn't paid for them, Jake learned to play the game. He got a job, earned money, said all the right things to our dad. I left my dorm and moved in with Clark. We both ended up the same…earning our own way. But it leaves a mark when someone you trust cheats you."

"It does." She caught his gaze. "Clark hadn't really cheated me, except for not putting my name on the condo. And I worry that when I tell this story to my parents, they're going to think I'm stupid."

"No. It might put another nail in their dislike of Clark, though."

She pulled in a breath. "So, how's your mom since your dad died?"

"Good." He frowned. "But we're not as close as I think she'd like us to be."

"Are you going to fix that?"

"A week ago, I would have said no." He shrugged. "Tonight, I don't know."

They both grew quiet. Harper looked at her watch and noticed the hour. "I better try to get some sleep. As soon as that gel wares off, Crystal will be up."

Seth flicked off the TV. "I'm going with you. I have to be up early tomorrow."

They headed down the hall, side by side. Quiet. Each lost in their own thoughts.

But when they reached her door, Seth stopped, too. "I know it hurt you that Clark kept so much a secret. But you've come out of this a very strong woman."

Pride shimmered through her. "Thanks."

She looked up as he looked down and the same temptation that always hit her when they were close eased through her. His eyes changed, went from happy to serious in a blink. Then he bent and kissed her.

The quick sweep of his mouth across hers raised gooseflesh but there was more to it than that. There was no surprise as there had been in the first kiss, no demand as there had been in the second kiss. Emotion warmed this kiss. Genuine affection. They'd gone from two people unexpectedly attracted, to two people who cared about each other and could talk to each other. She didn't have to be a psychic to realize Seth probably didn't talk about the fact that he and his mom weren't close.

Warmth filled her. Attraction blossomed in a new way, a more potent way. If she touched him now, it would be with affection, not curiosity. Which was stronger, more powerful. She'd give every cent she had to take away his pain over his dad, every cent she had to make him happy.

He pulled away, ran his thumb along her lower lip. "Hope you get at least an hour tonight."

She laughed. "I was kind of hoping for two."

He smiled. "Good night."

"Good night."

She watched him walk down the hall to his room, new feelings fluttering inside her.

He liked her.

He didn't feel sorry for her. Didn't feel he had to take care of her, be around her out of obligation.

He liked her.

CHAPTER TWELVE

THE NEXT MORNING Seth woke up and tiptoed past Harper's room, careful not to awaken either baby or mother. He took the Ferrari to work, rode the elevator to the McCallan executive floor and walked to his office, feeling the strangest things.

Happiness, of course. He'd helped Harper get her life back on track, and last night he'd talked her through her resentment about Clark. To do that, he'd had to tell her about his dad, but he hadn't hesitated.

And she'd understood.

Which filled him with something he could neither define nor describe.

He tried to analyze it. She might have understood because Clark had done something similar to what his dad had done. Clark's sins weren't nearly as egregious as his father's. But there was a common thread there that had given them an understanding of each other's situation.

He was just about positive that was why he'd

kissed her. And why the kiss had been so different, filled with emotion. What had started off as a light caress had formed a connection of some sort. Maybe a bond.

He'd forever remember Crystal's first tooth, remember Harper shopping for clothes, remember her struggling to right her life…and her listening about his dad.

It made him feel strange. Vulnerable in a way, but not really because he knew she'd never tell anyone. Not ever.

Which took him back to being happy.

Jake strolled into his office, a stack of contracts under his arm. "These are for you." He looked up from the contracts, saw Seth and frowned. "What's up with you?"

"Nothing's up with me."

"You have a silly look on your face."

"It's not a silly look. It's the expression of a guy who stayed up most of the night, listening for Crystal crying because she's getting a tooth."

"A tooth?" Jake laughed. "You are in for a lot of sleepless nights."

Worrying about Harper, he said, "How many?"

"I never counted Abby's, but it seemed like just

when one tooth would come in, another would start." He winced. "It's not fun."

"We can handle it," he said, without really thinking it through.

Jake studied him. "But you don't like babies. And you're not sleeping with Harper. What were they doing there?"

"She and the baby have been living with me since Harper's apartment sold. That's how we slid into dating." He decided to shift the conversation back to Crystal. "When you're living with a baby, you either grow to like her or figure out someplace else to sleep."

"So, you like her."

"Have you seen Crystal? She's cute as a bug." Realizing he sounded smitten, he added, "But if all goes well, I could be out of my condo in another few days. Two weeks at the most."

Jake took a seat in front of Seth's desk. "You found a place?"

"I did. A couple remodeled a penthouse then couldn't afford it. Everything's new. I offered top dollar."

"So you can leave your apartment?"

"No. So Harper can have an apartment...and

I can get a bigger place. Something more suited to my needs."

Jake frowned. "Are you breaking up with Harper?"

The question, though irrelevant because they weren't really dating, sent a shaft of confusion through him. What would they do when he moved out?

"We can still date."

Jake rose. "But you won't. Once you leave, I'm pretty sure you'll move on. Too bad." He nodded at the contracts on Seth's desk. "Legal team has those. They'll be briefing you in two weeks. It's your choice if you want to muddle through them now, then get their memorandums, or if you want to read the legal memos and then read the contracts."

Jake left Seth's office and he sat back in his chair, once again feeling strange.

It didn't seem right to leave Harper. Especially with Jake's prediction that once he moved out, he'd move on. Things weren't really settled for her. She might have had a good interview, but she didn't yet have a job.

He didn't have his new condo, either. As much

as he liked it, maybe he should hope the deal would fall through?

His phone rang. Bill Reynolds's name and smiling face popped up on his screen.

Harper awakened after eight. In the crib by the bed, Crystal slept soundly, which was natural, given that she'd cried from three to five.

Grateful both she and the baby had been able to fall back to sleep until eight, Harper walked to the kitchen to warm a bottle and make herself a cup of coffee.

There were a million things to think about today. First, if Seth got his penthouse, she would be moving in here. They hadn't talked about furniture, but she had her own. Not that she didn't like his, but he could use it until he bought new or even donate it to a charity.

That meant she had to get herself onto the schedule of a moving company. The last time she'd been lucky that the mover had had a cancellation. She couldn't count on that again.

She also needed to think about her job. If she got the position with Max, she'd need a babysitter, maybe day care. But after talking with Seth, realizing that his dad had been the worst parent possible, she had begun wondering if she should offer her mom the chance to keep Crystal one day a week.

It was strange to consider her mom for such a big job. But talking to Seth the night before had settled so much of her thinking. She understood that she could love Clark and not like some of the things he'd done in their marriage. She saw that her mom could be a heck of a lot worse, and that it was time to mend their relationship. Giving her a day with Crystal might be a good first step, if only because by offering she'd be telling her mom she trusted her.

Because she did. And she wanted her family back.

Her good mood increased, and she knew she owed that to Seth.

Thinking about him reminded her of their kiss at her bedroom door and her heart contracted. The three best kisses of her life had all been given to her by Seth.

Seth.

With his kindness, commitment to his brother and the family company, commitment to helping her—the widow of a friend—and his obvious love for her daughter, he was amazing.

Crystal began to cry, and Harper took the bottle from the water warming it. She checked the temperature on her wrist, approved it and raced into the bedroom.

"Hey, angel."

Crystal blinked up at her mom.

"Are you feeling better?"

The baby smiled.

"That's a very welcome smile."

She lifted Crystal from the crib, changed her and took her to the kitchen for her bottle. But when she was done eating, the baby glanced around, as if looking for something...someone.

"Oh, you're wondering where Seth is."

She gave her mother a sleepy-eyed smile.

"He's at work. And pretty soon your mom will be going to work, too." Although staying home with Crystal had much more appeal. She thought about the idea Sabrina had so easily tossed around: resurrecting her virtual-assistant company and staffing it with college kids. She wondered if the hundred and fifty thousand dollars she had in the bank was enough for startup capital and money to live on until the business got off the ground and decided she'd call Sabrina and ask her. Seth's sister wasn't just a smart woman; she counseled start-ups.

She picked up her phone just as it rang. Glancing at caller ID, she saw Max's company name. Shifting Crystal to her hip, she clicked on the call.

"Hello?"

"Hello, Harper. This is Julie at Max Wilson's office. I'm calling to let you know that if you still want the job as Max's assistant, it's yours."

Her plans for resurrecting her small business weren't clear enough yet to refuse a sure thing. "I want it."

"Good. You start next Monday. Report to Human Resources at eight."

"Okay. Thank you."

Happiness bubbled up inside her, as she disconnected the call. She shifted Crystal to her other hip and dialed her mom.

"Harper?"

"Yeah, it's me. I'm calling to tell you I got a job."

"Oh. Well, that's great?"

"It is great, Mom. I didn't tell you that Clark had mortgaged our condo and I had to sell it, or that he'd also leveraged the investment firm and I'd had to sell that, too."

"Oh."

The surprise in her mom's voice was expected. What was unexpected was the ease with which she could pour out the truth of her life to her. She'd thought this conversation would be hell. Instead, the truth flowed out naturally.

"He'd used the firm to as collateral to get a loan to buy Seth's share. The market fell right after he died, and I barely got enough when I sold it to pay off the loan."

"That's awful."

Harper's breath caught. Her mom had sympathized, and her voice sounded sincere.

"It was awful. Seth and I aren't really dating. He was letting me live here until I straightened everything out."

"He's a good guy." Her mother huffed out a sigh of disappointment, but didn't say anything about the charade. She let it drop as if she understood. "You should have called. Your dad and I could have helped you."

"I wanted to handle it on my own." And now she was glad she had. Very glad. She'd gotten herself out of debt and learned to trust again.

Seth helping her hadn't just staved off homelessness. It had given her back her faith in humanity.

She swallowed hard when that realization brought tears to her eyes.

He'd given her so much more than a place to stay.

"Anyway, I am totally on my feet now. But here's the interesting part. I thought maybe you'd like to take the baby one day a week. Not just because I'll be working, but because it would give you and Crystal a chance to get to know each other."

"Oh, Harper." The happy surprise in her mom's voice humbled her. "I'd love to."

"I'll have to find a daycare first. Then we'll talk specifics."

"That's fabulous. Your dad's going to be so thrilled."

"Thanks, Mom."

"You're welcome, sweetie."

"I have some more calls to make, so I'll talk to you once I know."

"Okay. I love you."

"I love you, too, Mom." Tears filled her eyes again as she hung up the phone. For the first time in eight years, she meant that.

* * *

When Seth arrived home for dinner, Harper had a feast waiting for him. "What happened?"

"What makes you think something happened?"

"You only go all out for dinner when you're nervous."

"I'm not nervous. I got the job."

His mouth fell open. Surprised and over-whelmingly pleased, he raced over, picked her up and swung her around. "That's great!"

"And I talked to your sister this afternoon about starting up my virtual-assistant business again. She says I can do it part-time for a year or two while I work for Max and see where it goes."

He looked up into her smiling face. "You've gone from no job to two jobs?"

"Yep."

He laughed and slid her down to the floor. He hadn't missed the easy way he'd caught her by the waist and lifted her up to swing her around. When she'd first come to his house, he'd never imagined they'd get this close. Yet here they were.

"I have a piece of news, too."

"Take off your jacket, wash your hands and sit down. You can tell me while we're eating."

"Okay."

He walked down the familiar hall to his bedroom, slipped out of the jacket and into the bathroom, where he washed his hands. Though Harper had never been in this room, everything about his condo seemed different tonight. Warm and cozy in the crispness of the October air. The scent of something Italian filling his nostrils. The sounds of cooing Crystal coming from the baby carrier sitting on the table.

"She sounds happy tonight."

"She is. The tooth isn't through by a long shot, but apparently babies get a break from the pain every once in a while. If you want to play with her after dinner, I would if I were you. We never know when the pain will be back."

Seth nodded, but sadness shot through him when he looked at Crystal and thought about how he'd soon be leaving.

Harper took her seat and handed him a spatula to dig out a helping of baked ziti. "Looks good."

"It's just one of those things I love to make." She smiled at him.

He watched her, his heart thrumming. He'd loved seeing her laugh with Sabrina at the cocktail party, thought there was no one more beautiful when she laughed...except she was more beautiful now. Contentment shone in her eyes. But also the light of expectation. She was securely on her new road in life now.

But so was he.

"I got the penthouse."

Her eyes widened. "Oh, Seth!" She bounced out of her seat and hugged him. "That's wonderful."

"Wonderful for both of us."

She returned to her seat, her head tilted. "More wonderful for you. I certainly want this condo and appreciate your generosity. But you wanted a new place to live, too."

He did. He loved that penthouse. "It's pretty awesome."

"Who doesn't love a kitchen fit for a caterer with a butler's pantry and a formal dining room?"

"I think more about a Christmas party in the huge living room with the lights of Manhattan as a backdrop."

Her eyes lit. "Can you imagine if it snows?"

"That would be cool."

"No, that would be ambiance."

He laughed and dug into his ziti, feeling a bit better about his move.

"What are you going to do about furniture?"

He took a bite of pasta, chewing as he thought about it. "This ziti is great."

"Thanks."

"I think I want to totally redecorate."

"Oh…that would be fun."

"Really?"

She playfully slapped his forearm. "Of course! I can almost see the beautiful rooms in my head and the possibilities."

He nearly asked her if she wanted to help him, then remembered that she had a full-time job, wanted to resurrect her assistant business and had a baby to care for.

He couldn't ask.

"I got the keys to the place today. It'll take a couple of weeks before it's officially mine, but because the owners are moved out and they happily cashed my check for the down payment, I got the key card to the elevator. The place is mine."

"That's great."

Harper had meant to say that with enthusiasm—instead her voice had faltered. Through all their weeks of planning for her to get a job and him to get a condo, they'd been hoping for this. Instead of being happy for them both, a thick, ugly sadness had planted itself in her chest.

"When does your job start?"

"Next Monday."

"Have you thought about daycare?"

"Already called. Four days a week she's in the daycare in the building of Max's company."

"Four?"

"One day a week she'll be with my mom. My dad's even thinking of taking the afternoon of that day off."

He sat back. "Wow."

"When I called her, my mom was confused at first about why I'd want a job, but I told her about Clark and the mortgage and leveraging the firm. Then I asked her if she wanted to babysit one day a week and she was happy." She bit her lip. "Actually, I told her I'd only been living with you. We weren't really dating."

"Oh." He didn't say anything for a few seconds, then he glanced across the table and caught her gaze. "How'd she take it?"

"It was barely a blip. I think she was so happy that I'd asked her to keep Crystal one day a week that she was stunned. I also think it's time for us to make up. To be a family again."

"So do I." He set his fork down. "It's like all your loose ends are tying up."

She nodded.

It felt right and yet wrong that she didn't need him anymore. Not that she wanted to depend on someone, more that it had been nice to share her burdens. Nice to have someone to talk to, someone to share her life with.

"When do you move into the penthouse?"

"I could go tonight."

She laughed, thinking he was kidding.

"I have a cot. Avery and Jake are meeting me at the house in the morning. Before work."

Her heart stumbled. "You're really leaving? Tonight?"

"It would be better to be sleeping there, so I'd be there when they arrive. Eventually, though, I'd have to come back for my things."

But by the time he got around to it, she'd already be working. He could come to the condo when she wasn't here, clear out his stuff, arrange for his furniture to be sent to a charity, and she'd never even see him.

Silence settled over the table. The ziti didn't seem so tasty anymore.

On the verge of tears, Harper noticed Crystal had fallen asleep in her carrier. "I better take her to the crib."

Seth's eyes took a slow trip over to Crystal. "Yeah. She looks beat."

"I wanted her to catch up on sleep today, but she wanted to play. Probably because she was feeling better."

"Maybe she'll sleep tonight."

"I hope."

She pulled the carrier off the table, but Seth suddenly rose. "Let me give her a kiss goodnight."

He walked over and bent down to press a soft kiss on Crystal's forehead, something he'd never done before.

Harper's chest expanded with love, then flattened with regret. It had taken him weeks to get adjusted to the baby and now he was leaving.

Probably tonight.

By the time she got the baby into bed and returned to the kitchen, he was scraping his ziti plate to put it into the dishwasher.

"You're leaving now?"

She said it like a question, but she knew what was happening. All news was out on the table. She had everything she had needed from him. He had his new penthouse, a place he was clearly excited to get to.

They were done.

Ask him to stay.

The words popped into her head as a soft suggestion. She looked at him closing the dishwasher door, and tried to will her mouth to move, but she couldn't. She was the one who'd told him nothing romantic could happen between them.

But he was the one who'd told her he wasn't the guy to settle down with. He was the guy to experiment with.

She'd worked too hard and too long to get her life back in order. Wouldn't asking him to stay be like messing it up again?

Seth walked back to his bedroom, grabbed his jacket and a prepacked bag he had ready for spur-of-the-moment out-of-town trips and headed up the hall again.

Harper wore a strained smile. He knew what she was thinking—their change of fortune had happened too fast. He really didn't have to leave but even he saw the handwriting on the wall. A moment of weakness would be awful for them both. He'd told her his terms. He didn't do permanent, but he did do fun. If they got soft again with each other tonight, shared more secrets, another kiss, they'd end up in bed. He had to leave now—

Unless she understood that sleeping together didn't mean anything except a moment of happiness for both of them?

Ask me to stay.

He willed the wish across the room. Not so much because he wanted to sleep with her but because he wanted another night. Being vulnerable with her had been exquisite. He'd never shared so many of his secrets with anyone. Mostly because he knew other people wouldn't understand. She had understood. They'd talked things out. Both her troubles and his.

Now he just wanted one night of real closeness. If the sadness on her face was anything to go by, she wanted it, too.

"You know you don't have to go."

That wasn't what he wanted to hear from her. And she knew it. She had to ask him to stay, not tell him he didn't have to leave. He couldn't ask her. He'd already asked once. She had to say it.

Ask me to stay.

She pressed her lips together and stepped back. Shakily. "Okay, if you need anything…"

Disappointment tumbled through him. "I can call."

She nodded.

He looked into her pretty blue eyes, stalling to give her another ten seconds to change her mind. When she didn't, he headed for the door.

Regret tried to fill him, except part of the reason he liked her was her honesty. The sweet, sweet knowledge that she'd never lie to him, never manipulate him, only tell him the truth. She wanted more than he could give. He had to accept that.

He opened the door. Stepped out in the hall. Almost knocked on Mrs. P.'s door to say goodbye, but he thought better of it.

As much as this hurt, he needed the clean break, or he'd pine after her for weeks, maybe months, the way he'd done after Clark asked her out and she'd accepted.

CHAPTER THIRTEEN

SETH AWOKE THE next day to the sound of the house phone. Knowing only the doorman had the number, he raced to get it.

"Yes?"

"Your brother and sister-in-law are here."

"Send them up."

He slid into jeans and a big T-shirt and got to the great room just in time to see the elevator open and his brother and Avery step out.

Avery said, "Wow."

Jake agreed. "It's huge and gorgeous."

"Can you see the parties here?"

Jake laughed, but Avery walked around nodding. "Elegant parties."

"I'm not sure about elegant. I'm still young enough to be a little bad." But in his head, he saw what Avery saw: the room as neat as a pin, with sofas and tables, flowers and a fire in the fireplace, and the backdrop view. All because he had other rooms. A den. An office. A room that could be a playroom. A master suite big enough to have a nursery beside it.

He sucked in a breath. He knew why he'd had the thought, but he blocked it. He and Harper were not a good match.

The house phone rang again.

Jake winced. "I forgot to mention that I invited Mom. We had dinner together last night. I told her you'd bought a new place and somehow she wheedled it out of me that Avery and I were seeing it before work."

"It's okay." He picked up the phone. "If that's my mom, send her up."

Avery and Jake poked around in the butler's pantry, kitchen and dining room while his mother rode up in the elevator. When they heard the doors open, they returned to the great room.

"This is amazing," his mother said as she glanced around. "So much room." She faced Seth. "You have the entire top floor?"

"Gorgeous views from every room."

She nodded sagely. "Good for resale value."

He wished he could do what Harper had done. Come clean with his mom and get a fresh start. But Harper hadn't suffered humiliation, as he had. And his mom had turned a blind eye. How did they talk about that? Forgive that?

He turned toward the butler's pantry. "Wait until you see the rest of the place."

He took them through the kitchen area, dining room, guest bath, two guest bedrooms, the master suite and then another two guest suites.

"It's huge." His mother gaped at the view from the second guest suite. "Big enough for a family of six."

Jake laughed, but Seth shot him a withering look.

Jake only smiled, looked at his watch and caught Avery's elbow. "We have to go."

She glanced at her phone. "Yes, we do." She walked over and kissed Seth's cheek. "It's a lovely home. I'm sure you will enjoy it immensely."

When they were gone, Seth suddenly realized he was alone with his mother. Misery nagged at him. He had so many questions.

His mother put her hands on her hips. "What are you doing?"

Hoping she couldn't read his mind, he said, "Showing off the house I've always wanted."

"Where's Harper?"

Harper. He'd spent the night fighting thoughts of her. Thoughts of Paris. Thoughts of propositioning her and her not wanting what he wanted. Feelings had bubbled up, spilled over. But in the end, he'd done the best he could for her.

"Right now, I'm guessing she's enjoying the condo I'm giving her for cost."

Her eyes narrowed, and she made a sound of disgust. "Really?"

"You don't like that I'm not charging her interest?"

"I don't like that she's not here, helping you plan, talking about decorating this place, talking about a wedding."

Seth groaned inwardly. Now, he understood. And since Harper had come clean with her mom, he could come clean with his. "Mom, Harper and I were only dating because she had financial problems she didn't want her parents to know about. She'd sold her condo and didn't have time to get another. She would have been on the street, if I hadn't helped her."

She shook her head. "You like her. Maybe even love her."

He sniffed. "Where in the hell would you come up with an idea like that?"

She walked up to him and scrutinized his face. "From your eyes."

He turned away.

"You bought a house with a nursery attached to the master."

"Some people might look at that and see a reading room."

She tossed her hands in despair. "Seriously. You love that girl and she loves you. What is wrong with you?"

He spun around to face his mother. "How dare you ask me what's wrong with me when you know damned well why I think marriage is a sham! You and dad had the worst marriage in the world. He should have left you if he wanted every woman he looked at, or you should have kicked him out and saved your pride. Instead, you lived together like two miserable inmates in a prison…"

She gasped. "Seth!"

"It's true!"

"Okay. I'm going to let you get away with insulting me and your father since I've never talked about any of this with you. But this conversation is once and only this once. The truth is I tried to leave your father twice, but I had this crazy thought in my head that even a bad father was better than no father."

"I think we all know that's not true."

"Do you think he wouldn't have tormented you from a distance if I'd moved you out of his home? Of course, he would have. But first he would have told you lies about me. Your father was a miserable human being who would have used you, Jake and Sabrina as pawns. I knew it. No matter what I'd said or done, he would have ruined you three. As it was, he got a shot at you but not with the big ammunition he would have had if I'd left him and filed for divorce. He would have never accepted a divorce. A black mark. A failure. Everyone did his bidding or they suffered."

The air backed up in Seth's lungs. He'd never considered that his mean, manipulative father wouldn't have accepted a divorce. But why would he? Why should he? He was vindictive. Cruel. Sometimes, Seth even believed his dad had enjoyed being cruel.

Even if his mom would have left, his dad would have had visitation rights, maybe even filed for custody. He would have tormented them with lies about their mother. He would have tormented them period.

He rubbed his hands down his face.

"Do you understand?"

"Yes." Because his dad was a miserable human being. A master manipulator. A liar. "You stayed with him to save us from the third level of hell."

"Essentially, yes. But, Seth, not all marriages are like that. Look at Jake and Avery. They're happy. Not only that, very few people are like your father. Especially not Harper."

He sucked in a breath.

"She'd make you so happy." She shook her head. "No. She's already made you happy. You're calmer, content. When I heard you were looking for a new place, maybe even a house in Connecticut, I was sure you were nesting, making a home."

When Seth said nothing, she walked over to him. "I know you saw a lot of things a little boy shouldn't see. I'm sorry for that. But if you walk away from Harper because of your father, he wins again. He doesn't just strip you of your childhood or make your adolescence miserable, he steals your life. Your love. Your first real chance for happiness."

With that she turned and walked to the elevator, her footsteps echoing around him, reminding him of how empty his life had been until Harper moved in.

He glanced around at the huge room that Harper wanted to see decorated at Christmas, thought of the room in the master suite that could be a nursery and wondered if his subconscious didn't agree with his mom—

He'd bought this place for the family he so desperately wanted.

Harper's cell phone rang far too early. She looked at the time, saw it was close to ten and tossed off the bedcovers. A quick peek in the direction of Crystal's crib showed she was still sleeping. The baby had fallen asleep after her seven o'clock feeding and so had Harper. She'd tossed and turned the night before, miserable and alone without Seth.

She answered the phone with a groggy "Hello."

"Hey, it's me."

Seth.

Her heart broke all over again. He was probably calling to tell her about arrangements he'd made for his furniture or clothes.

"I'm still at the penthouse. I have a decorator coming around noon, and I wondered—"

"If I'd meet with her?" Her vision clouded with tears. She should say no. It was better not to see someone you wanted but couldn't have. But she couldn't take the quick separation. She needed to wean herself away from him. Needed to see him at least one more time. And even if he wasn't there while she met with the decorator, she'd have to tell him about their meeting. Maybe he'd even come here to talk?

"Sure. I'd be happy to meet with her. You go ahead to work."

"Actually, I'm going to be here, too."

Her heart jumped at the chance to see him. "Okay. I can be there at noon."

"How about eleven thirty?"

"I'll need to call Mrs. Petrillo…"

"You have plenty of time. I'll have one of the limos downstairs to meet you at eleven fifteen so you're here at eleven thirty."

That surprised her, but given that this was such short notice, it made sense. "Okay."

She drank her coffee, showered and dressed before Crystal woke.

When her little girl was fed, she walked her

to Mrs. Petrillo's door. The older woman took the baby with an expression of glee and Harper headed downstairs.

She found the limo just as Seth had said and took it to his new building. She walked inside and found the doorman.

"I'm Harper Hargraves."

He handed her the key card to the elevator. "Mr. McCallan said to give you this."

She almost winced. There was only one reason he'd give her the elevator key. As much as she liked him and wanted to remain friends, she couldn't take charge of decorating his entire penthouse. She knew what would happen. At some point, her willpower would disappear, and they'd sleep together…and he'd tire of her.

That was bitter reality.

She took the elevator to the top floor. The doors opened automatically. She stepped out into the echoing great room.

"Seth?"

"Over here."

He stood by the wall of windows, looking at Manhattan.

"I know you called me here because—"

He turned from the window, caught her gaze. "I love you."

Her heart stopped. Her breathing stopped. But she was positive that she hadn't heard correctly, so she said, "What?"

"I love you. I realized it last night. I wanted to stay, but you wouldn't ask me."

His words paralyzed her. Not because she didn't believe him. Because she did. He was too sensitive, too serious to lie about something so important.

Still, he might love her, but he couldn't make a commitment. And she needed a commitment—something. Even if it was just that they would live together.

"Seth, I get that you have feelings for me. But we discussed this." She shook her head. "You told me that you're not the guy who settles down. You're the guy to experiment with."

He had the audacity to laugh. "Things change."

Disbelief made her shake her head again. "Just like that?"

He got down on one knee. Pulled a ring box from his jeans pocket.

Her breath stuttered.

"I want to marry you."

She stared at the beautiful emerald cut diamond. "Oh, Seth." She wanted to believe him. But even as her heart leaped for joy, her common sense shuddered with vulnerability. "A person doesn't change overnight."

Still on one knee, he laughed again. "My mother tells me I've been changing since the day you moved in."

She could almost believe that because she'd been falling in love with him bit by bit since she first saw him standing in his doorway, yanking a T-shirt over his pecs and abs.

"But the truth is I loved you before Clark. I've loved you since I moved in next door to you. I let Clark ask you out because I knew I was damaged goods."

She kneeled in front of him, pressed her palms to his cheeks. "You're not damaged goods."

"I was. For the longest time I was. I thought I couldn't settle down, thought kids were scary, thought I'd hurt any woman who loved me." He caught her gaze. "You changed all that."

She whispered, "I did?"

"You accepted me for who I was, wasn't afraid to push me to do the duties a good friend should do and kiss like nobody I've ever kissed before."

She laughed. "It has been different."

"An adventure." He kissed her, light and brief, a promise of things to come. Then he presented the ring box to her. The gorgeous emerald cut diamond winked at her.

"Want to see where this adventure goes?"

Happy tears pooled in her eyes. She threw her arms around him. "Yes!"

The phone rang. "Good, because that call is probably the doorman telling me the decorator is here."

He stood up, reached down and helped her to rise. "I love you."

"I know." She searched his eyes, finding only truth and sincerity there. "I love you, too."

"Well, there you go. It certainly took you long enough to say it."

The house phone rang again. He strode over to answer it. "Hello." He winked at her during the pause. "Send her up."

"Ready to make this place a home?"

She stood on her tiptoes and kissed him. "Absolutely."

He caught her waist, hauled her to him and kissed her deeply. Her chest tightened. Her stomach tingled and everything inside of her suddenly wished they were back at the old condo with no decorator coming and a perfectly good bed, where they could try out this new love that they'd found.

The sound of the elevator door made them draw apart. Seth slid his hand around her waist and greeted the tall, slender woman.

"Mrs. Green?"

She walked over, hand extended. "Yes. It's nice to meet you. And this must be—"

"My fiancée."

A huge smile broke out on Harper's face, not just because he hadn't hesitated but because she loved him and he was hers.

Forever.

EPILOGUE

THEY MARRIED ALMOST two years later. Their August wedding was filled with lilac and pink, and a beige gown for the red-haired maid of honor, Avery. Crystal, two years old now, served as flower girl alongside Abby, who was nearly three years old—both wore pink.

Sabrina McCallan watched as Harper walked up the long aisle of the cathedral, her exquisite jeweled veil flowing behind her. Her mom's veil. Because it was so fancy, Harper had chosen a simple satin dress with cap sleeves and a skirt that eased out at the waist, into a long layer of satin that formed a train.

Sabrina's brother, Seth, watched his bride with love in his eyes. He looked good in his tux, and Sabrina had to admit she knew they were a perfect match. The beautiful waif and her handsome, strong, knight in shining armor.

Harper's father finished the walk up the aisle

with his daughter and as he handed her off to Seth, Sabrina saw the tears in his eyes.

Then Harper and Seth stood before the pastor to say their vows and promise to love each other forever. Crystal fussed at the end of the ceremony and Harper stopped and scooped her into her arms before she and Seth walked down the aisle out of the church.

Jake and Avery, best man and maid of honor, also stopped to get Abby. Avery looked amazing in the pretty pale dress, even with her six-month-pregnant belly.

Before Trent Sigmund, aka Ziggy, her brother's best friend and Sabrina's groomsman partner, could turn to walk her out of the church, Sabrina looked down at her own stomach. Six weeks along. That's what her doctor had said. She blew her breath out in a long, slow stream. In this family of people who loved kids, she was about to bring her own child into the fold.

Except she wasn't married.

And the baby's father didn't know.

And she had no idea where his globe-trotting behind was…

* * * * *

LET'S TALK
Romance

For exclusive extracts, competitions
and special offers, find us online:

f facebook.com/millsandboon

◎ @millsandboonuk

𝕏 @millsandboon

Or get in touch on 0844 844 1351*

For all the latest titles coming soon,
visit millsandboon.co.uk/nextmonth

Want even more
ROMANCE?

Join our bookclub today!

'Mills & Boon books, the perfect way to escape for an hour or so.'

Miss W. Dyer

'Excellent service, promptly delivered and very good subscription choices.'

Miss A. Pearson

'You get fantastic special offers and the chance to get books before they hit the shops'

Mrs V. Hall

Visit millsandbook.co.uk/Bookclub and save on brand new books.

MILLS & BOON